The WALTON BOYS

and

Gold in the Snow

By HAL BURTON

Illustrated by
ROBERT DOREMUS

WHITMAN PUBLISHING COMPANY
RACINE, WISCONSIN

Contents

1   *The Mystery of the Map*

Bert Walton snapped shut the dusty volume of *Oliver Twist,* automatically ran one hand through his unruly red hair, and raced for the dining room, shouting, "Hey, Dad! Look what I found!"

As he burst through the door, he clutched in his right fist a yellowed piece of paper. He could see his father, mother and two brothers looking up at him with startled faces from their chairs around the massive dining-room table.

"It's—it's a map, Dad," he concluded in a calmer tone of voice. His freckled face flushed with embarrassment as he realized that he'd violated one of the cardinal rules of the Walton family—"Never raise your voice." He sensed an unspoken reproach in his father's eyes as he flattened the map on the linen tablecloth and strove to control his excitement.

"Excuse me, Mom," he said hastily to his mother. "But, gosh! I've got a good reason for being excited. I think I've found the map of Uncle John's missing gold mine!"

"No kidding, Bert?" asked his younger brother, Howard. "But are you really sure it's Uncle John's map—not just a fake?"

"Quiet, small fry!" Bert growled in mock anger. "Don't forget that I'm entitled to respect from you. I'm fourteen, and you're only thirteen, you know." He leaned eagerly toward his father. "Look, Dad. Doesn't it look like a real old map to you? All yellow, and with faded ink and dusty, too, as if—"

"First tell us how you happened to find it," broke in the voice of his older brother, Ed. At sixteen, he commanded the respect of both younger boys for his steadiness and good judgment. Bert turned his attention from his father to speak directly to Ed.

"You remember that old set of Dickens that's been kicking around down cellar?" he asked his older brother. "Well, today in school my teacher told us that *Oliver Twist* was to be required reading for this term. I tried to borrow it at the library, but they only had two copies, and those were already spoken for.

"So then I remembered that we had a lot of old books in the cellar—some of those from Uncle John's library, and I thought I might as well look through them to see if *Oliver Twist* was among them. Sure enough, it was."

"And?" prompted his father.

"Well, I came upstairs and started to read," Bert said. "But the book was awful dusty and I couldn't find a cloth to clean it with. So I just grabbed it by the binding and shook it, and this map dropped out."

As he pulled a chair up to the table, he watched the gleam of interest in his father's eye. His attention was so closely fixed that he caught the doubting look Mr. Walton suddenly cast at Howard and his father's half-stern inquiry.

"Now, Howard, are you sure this isn't just another one of your practical jokes?"

Bert sighed audibly as Howard answered with unaccustomed seriousness, "Gee, no, Dad! I hardly knew those books were down cellar. You know me— I never get any closer to a book than I can help."

Dinner was forgotten, and the roast of beef that lay on a platter in front of Mr. Walton cooled in its own juices as Bert carefully listened to his father's analysis of the map.

"That's a road," he heard his father say as he pointed at

two parallel lines. "The arrow down here points to Salt Lake City, so this area must be somewhere to the south of there. You see, the arrow points north. Here's a dotted line—a trail, I guess. And here, up on the corner where it says 'Avalanche Creek' is an 'X' and the printed word, 'Mine.' And down here in the valley, where the map shows a brook, is the name of a town, so faded it's hard for me to read without my glasses. Bert, you've got sharp eyes. What do you make of it?"

"Sunmount, Dad," Bert said softly, flicking his blue eyes toward the map and then back toward his father. He caught immediately the look of amazement on Mr. Walton's face, and his heart leaped as his father leaned back and stroked his chin reflectively.

"Well, I'll be darned!" he said softly. "Maybe there *is* something to this old map."

"Do you mean we might be rich?" asked Bert hopefully.

"I don't know about that," his father said to him, "but I'll tell you the story. You've never heard the whole thing. Long ago your great-uncle John, my uncle, told me about a gold-mining claim he had staked out in the West.

"He was an old man by then, and he wasn't very specific about it. I really thought his mind must be wandering. I knew he had traveled in the West and had transacted some business out there, but I didn't take him too seriously.

"He used to say to me, 'Boy, just read enough books, and someday you'll be rich. Just keep on reading, boy; keep on reading.' "

"Well, Dad, you did read enough law books to do pretty well for yourself," said Bert, grinning.

"Yes," said Mr. Walton, "that's what I assumed. Uncle John knew I wanted to be a lawyer; and, of course, I figured he was talking about law books. But, you know, it's just barely possible that he hid this map in *Oliver Twist* before he died and expected me to find it. As it happened, I wasn't much interested in Dickens, and when your mother and I were married, we stored the books down cellar because we didn't have space in the library."

"Try and think if he told you anything else about the mine," Howard urged.

"Well, come to think of it, he did," his father answered. "He said the mine was in a mountain range out in Utah, but that it wasn't registered at the State Capitol. I seem to recall his saying that he'd hired a prospector to go in with a pickax and see what he could find. The prospector wrote him he couldn't find anything. Uncle John was inclined to be a suspicious fellow, and he didn't believe the prospector's story. As a matter of fact, I thought Uncle John had imagined the whole thing, or that he was playing another practical joke. He liked to kid people, just as Howard here does."

"But you don't think this a joke, do you, Dad?" asked Bert.

"I don't know *what* to think now," said his father. "But if it will make you any happier, tomorrow I'll get in touch with a firm of lawyers out in Salt Lake City. I'll even phone them and tell them about the map and see what they have to say."

Grinning from ear to ear, Bert stood up and carefully carried his chair over to the other end of the table, where he always sat during meals. As he waited for his plate to come back, heaped with a slice of roast, potatoes, and carrots, he stared thoughtfully out the window.

Throughout dinner it was obvious he had something other than dinner on his mind. When his mother rang the bell that signaled the end of the course, and Mary, the maid, walked through the swinging door from the kitchen, he leaned forward, propped his elbows on the table, and waited to catch his father's eye.

"Dad," he said, "supposing this *is* true, and supposing there *is* such a mine, can Ed and Howard and I go out and look for it?"

His brothers stared at him with new interest as he waited for his father's reply.

"I'll make a bargain with you," his father said. "It has a couple of 'ifs' in it. You boys are interested in skiing, and I want you to be good skiers. So *if* you place in the first ten in the high school downhill race this week end, and *if* your principal at school is willing to give you a week's leave of absence after Easter vacation, and *if* there is the slightest chance that this map is actually genuine, then—" he paused.

"Then what, Dad?" cried Bert excitedly.

"Then I'll let you go out there to look for the mine," his father finished. "You may not find anything, but from what little I know of Utah, you'll certainly get some good skiing."

"And the season will be finished here, anyway," said Bert, sitting back in his chair again. "What could be more perfect, fellas? A vacation skiing in Utah—powder snow— wonderful open slopes—just like that booklet from Utah I saw up at the ski club cabin the other day.

"Boy," he said, half to himself. "I'm going to walk on

tiptoe until it's time for the race. Don't want anything to happen to me."

The sound of chairs being pushed back roused him from his reverie, and he heard Ed saying, "Come on, kid. Let's wax our skis. Remember, we've only a half day's school tomorrow, and then we're all allowed to go practice for the race."

Bert jumped up hastily, kissed his mother a quick good night, nodded to his father, and said to his brothers, "Okay. Let's go. First one down cellar gets a chance to use the waxing table first."

He sprinted for the kitchen, almost bowling over Mary as he sped past the stove, and then started down the cellar steps two at a time. He didn't hear Mary's warning cry, nor did he know what had happened until, with a clatter that shook the house, he tumbled headlong down the steps.

An agonizing pain shot through his left leg as he tried to lift himself from a tangle of pots, pans, and a mammoth tin laundry tub on which he had tripped. The cellar light flashed on, and he looked up into the solicitous faces of his brothers.

"Are you hurt badly?" he heard Ed ask.

"No, it's nothing—just pulled a muscle, I guess."

He tried to rise and then sank back again, mumbling that his left ankle hurt. Footsteps sounded on the stairway. It was his father.

"I'm—I'm all right, Dad," he said weakly. "Just a little sprain."

He grasped at the stair railing and painfully pulled himself upright. It took all his will power to rest his weight evenly on both feet. The ankle had begun to throb, and its pounding seemed to echo in his head as he forced a smile.

Ed's arm was around him as he hobbled to the waxing table, a long trestle set on two wooden horses, with a hole in the middle into which the skis could fit with their bindings when turned upside down for waxing. He looked gratefully at Ed, and drew forward his skis from the back of the table.

Resting his weight on his uninjured right foot with his left foot raised off the floor, he opened a tube of ski wax and began to rub it with long, sweeping strokes from the tip to the tail of the skis. Next, using a square chunk of cork, he carefully worked the wax into the soles of the skis until there was an even, glistening film for the full length. The throbbing in his ankle had subsided a little, but it still hurt.

"Ed," he said, turning to his older brother, "maybe you'd

better tape this ankle. Don't tell Dad, but it still hurts a lot."

He hobbled to an old chair and stretched out his leg. Ed's skilled fingers unlaced his shoe, removed his sock, and pressed gently on the flesh at the sides of his ankle. As Howard could see, the ankle was beginning to swell. Bert winced a little, involuntarily, as Ed carefully wound adhesive tape over the swelling and then finished with some vertical strips of tape.

"Don't worry," he said to his brothers. "I'll race." Using the railing for balance, he carefully lifted himself up the stairs. As he opened the kitchen door, he forced himself to walk with even steps past Mary's appraising eyes, through the dining room, and up the stairs to his bedroom.

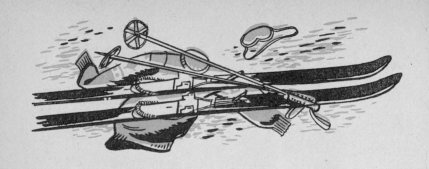

2   *Bert Walton's Toughest Race*

In the Saturday morning sun the mountain glittered like a huge, frosted cake. As Mr. Walton skillfully swung the car around the curves and up the final hill to the ski center, Bert stole a look at the clock on the dashboard. Nine o'clock. Time for at least two practice runs before lunch, and then at two o'clock, the race. He felt a fluttery feeling in his stomach—the same feeling he always had when he knew that he would soon be standing at the top of the mountain, ski bindings parallel with the poles that marked the starting line, feeling the timer's hand on his shoulder, and hearing a voice call off the final seconds, "Five, four, three, two, one, GO!"

Before he could mentally drop down the first steep strip of snow, the car slowed and Mr. Walton, looking quizzically at him, said, "Okay, Bert. Here we are. Do your best

—and try to win. I'm rooting for all of you."

"We'll all be trying to win, Dad," Bert assured him as he pulled down the door latch and swung out to the ground. He had almost forgotten about his bad ankle, and he stepped down a little too abruptly. A spasm of pain that he could not control flickered across his face, but Mr. Walton had his head turned toward the two boys in the back seat. As they joined Bert on the ground, Mr. Walton tossed a last message at them.

"Remember, all of you, if you place in the first ten, you'll go to Utah—that is, if my phone call this morning turns up any information. All of you boys have a habit of starting things and then not finishing them. Remember your bird collection, Bert? And your job last summer, Howard? And your short-wave radio set, Ed?"

The three boys nodded acknowledgment, and their father continued, "This time, let's see you really finish something—finish the race; and, what's more, try to win it. I'll phone out to let you know what I hear from Utah." The exhaust pipe of his car let out a puff of vapor as he stepped on the accelerator, swung around, and shifted into high gear. Skis resting against their crooked elbows, the three boys looked thoughtfully after him.

"We've got to win," burst out Bert. His brothers soberly nodded acknowledgment as they shouldered their skis and walked over toward the foot of the trail. They noticed, but did not comment on, Bert's noticeable limp. At the foot of the trail all three carefully placed their skis on the snow, kicked their boots into the toeplates, adjusted the steel cable hitch to its loosest point to allow free movement of their heels as they climbed.

As they sidestepped upward, there came from above a warning cry of "Track!" and a trim figure in tapered trousers, a gray parka and a visored cap came diving down over the top of the schuss. The boys separated to let him pass, and then craned their necks to watch as he gracefully swung his weight and sped around the corner below in a parallel turn.

"That's the guy we've got to beat," said Bert. "Ollie Johnson. He's hot today. Did you see him take that turn? Close in, just shaving the trees, as straight as he could."

"Yeah," said Howard. "And if you hadn't gone and sprained your ankle, you'd be the one to beat him. You seem to forget that I'm more of a jumper than I am a downhill racer, and Ed is best in cross-country and *slalom*. It's up to you, Bert."

"I'll do my best," Bert promised, "but this ankle still hurts a lot."

The shelter cabin was filled with laughing, talking youngsters and the odor of wet, snowy clothing. Frost lay thick on the windows, and outside the trees were coated with it. Every now and then a youngster looked at the clock on the wall, swallowed, and quietly walked out the door, which opened to let in a gust of cold air and then closed again. The race had begun, and every racer was trying to forget about the clock until his time came to leave.

Bert sat with his leg propped on a bench, talking to his brothers and tying the strings to the cloth bib with a number 24 on it—his racing number. Racer 21 had just stepped out the door. Bert looked at his brothers, winked, and said, "I'll see you at the bottom."

"Not before!" Howard warned him. "I'm twenty-five and Ed is twenty-six, and we don't want to run you down."

"Don't worry about running me down," said Bert sharply. "And don't stop for anything. If I don't win, I want you fellows to."

He raised himself stiffly and hobbled out the door, where his skis lay parallel on the snow. He stepped into the bindings and adjusted the cables to their highest tension.

As he slid toward the starting line, he suddenly remembered he hadn't heard from Dad about the call to Utah. Well, that could wait. He nervously readjusted the straps of his ski poles. One of them was cutting into his left wrist. He tested the strength of the knot in the string that kept his ski cap on his head. Then he stepped into position between the starting poles as number twenty-three pushed off in a cloud of snow. The starter was his old friend, Charley Lowell, the hardware man.

"Have a good time," said Charley reassuringly.

"He's great," Bert thought. "Tries to keep everybody's mind off their troubles." He felt Charley's hand on his shoulder and could sense that Charley was looking at his stop watch.

"Five," said Charley. "Four . . . three . . . two . . . one . . . GO!"

Bert shoved off into space. He could feel the snow drop away beneath him, and for the moment he almost forgot the dull, pervasive pain in his left ankle. Down—down— he was going pretty fast. He'd better put in a turn to cut down his speed. Months of training had taught him to react automatically. A turn to the right and then another to the left would cut him down to thirty miles an hour, and he would be in full control of his skis.

The ankle pained badly as he brought most of the weight of his body over the left-hand ski, and he quickly began the counterswing for a turn to the other direction. That was easier to do. The snow sprayed out behind him as he completed the rhythm of the turn—the counterswing, the reversing of weight, the delicate rotary movement of the body, and then the forward lean and the deep forward bending of the knees as he straightened out in the finish of the turn. He could afford to hold down on his speed a little here; he could make time on the Railroad Schuss and lower down where the trail was flatter. Ahead of him and just on a corner, a sycamore tree loomed up. He swung by it, his shoulder almost grazing the rough bark.

"Ouch!" he thought, as his skis skidded a little. "That corner's icy. I'll bet the corners down below are just as icy. I'd better take them a little wider."

Down he dropped, through straightaways, around S turns. "The runner ahead must have finished," he thought to himself. "And I've got to finish, too, before Howard starts. There's just a two-minute leeway between racers."

Now he was dropping down over snow dappled with

sunlight, great spruce trees hanging overhead. The Railroad Schuss was just around the corner.

"Let her go, boy," he said to himself. "This is where you make time."

The top of the Railroad Schuss rushed toward him. It was so steep that he could look out into space and miles across the valley to the glittering windows and the white houses of the village. As the slope suddenly dropped away from him, he dove forward and deepened his crouch. The trees seemed to close in. Then, far down the slope, he saw a figure in the snow, struggling to rise. It was the racer who had started before him!

"If he only moves in time!" Bert thought agonizedly. "And if he doesn't—I'm out of the race. There's hardly room to pass. If I don't fall, I'll have to check so hard that I'll lose every bit of speed I've made."

Grimly he kept his skis together. The racer below him struggled to his feet. Less than three yards separated them— and then slowly, painfully, the racer moved out of the way. Where he had fallen was a gaping hole. Bert held his breath and plunged into it. As he came out the other side of the hole, he flew into the air. He landed with a resounding smack, but still upright on his skis. And then he remembered. The sharpest curve of all was just ahead.

"I can't make it," he told himself. Deliberately he leaned back. As his shoulders hit the snow, he spun over and over again, half-rolling, half-bouncing. He could see tree trunks whirling by him, but miraculously he was safe and half-buried in a drift of snow. It took him a minute to get his breath; then he carefully placed his two ski poles on the upper side of his body, pushed up and forward, and rose on his skis. One of them, he could see, was intact. The other seemed to be buried in a mound of snow. He pulled it backward gingerly, and a pang of disappointment shot through him. The right ski had broken off neatly, just in front of the binding. He was out of the race.

Resting his weight on his left ski, despite the pain it caused him, he slid over to the trail. He couldn't use the right ski at all. It would only catch and trip him.

"Doesn't matter," he said to nobody in particular. "A good racer always finishes, even if he has to finish on foot."

Sliding, falling along the edge of the trail, he began his nightmare descent. He saw Howard flash by, his eyes fixed on the race course, and he shouted reassuringly to his younger brother. Two minutes later came Ed, graceful as ever, poised as he acknowledged Bert's hoarse greeting by waving a ski pole for a second.

It seemed hours later when the flags at the finish line loomed up in front of him. Between him and the finish was one last, steep schuss.

"Here goes nothing," he said to himself and shot over the edge. He lit sprawling at the bottom, almost too tired to care. But with one last burst of flagging energy, he raised himself again and slowly, painfully, slid across the finish line. As he lay there, he heard a burst of applause, and then strong arms lifted him to his feet. Somebody pushed a cup of bouillon into his hands. As he sucked down the steaming broth, he felt an arm on his shoulder. It was his father.

"Never mind, boy," said Mr. Walton. "As far as I'm concerned, you won that race on sportsmanship and guts. It doesn't matter how you placed."

"That's right," broke in Ellis Meldrow, the chief timer. "We're giving you an honorary first place, and we'll have an extra medal struck off for you."

A grin spread over Bert's tired face. He winked at his brothers, who by now had kicked off their skis and had run up to shake hands with him.

"You mean that I finished something I started for a change, Dad?" he asked.

"You bet you did," said his father. "And so did your brothers. The judges tell me they'll be in the first ten."

"Then what about Utah?" Bert asked eagerly. His father pulled a scrap of paper from his pocket.

"According to my notes," he said, "there is a strong chance that Uncle John's mine actually *does* exist. That's item one. Item two: Your principal says you have sufficiently good marks so that he'll let you take a leave of absence immediately following Easter vacation. Item three: Your plane leaves from Boston at eight tomorrow morning."

There was a shout of, "Wow!" and the three brothers clustered together, slapping each other on the back. For a moment, they forgot their father.

"And, boys," his voice reminded them, "if you find the mine, it's yours—all of it, and all the gold that's in it."

Airborne for Utah

The airlines limousine, sleek and glistening, slid to a stop in front of the terminal building at Boston Airport. As Bert looked out through the window, he could see a grinning Negro porter move forward to swing open the doors. From the seat ahead of him, he heard Ed's voice.

"Here we are, fellows," his brother said. "Be careful getting out. We don't want any more sprained ankles."

Bert grinned wryly as he pulled up one trouser leg and inspected the lumpy mass of tape that swathed his left ankle.

"Don't worry, bud," he replied. He slid deftly out of his seat, extended his right leg stiffly, and let it take the full weight of his body.

Ed and Howard had bounded out and were busily conferring with the porter, who swung open the rear compartment of the limousine and began to take out skis, suit-cases and rucksacks jammed with clothes.

"We'll get your stuff, Bert," they called over their shoulders. "Go on in." As Bert walked toward the swinging doors at the entrance of the terminal, he could see the porter staggering under the load.

"You boys must really be travelin'," his voice floated back.

Howard's high tenor replied, "You bet we are—all the way to Utah!"

A tall, dark-haired youngster, striding just ahead of Bert, swung around sharply as he heard the phrase, and Bert had to stop abruptly to keep from bumping into him. He could see surprise and interest mingled on the stranger's dark, sullen face.

"Excuse me," Bert said politely, and the stranger stepped back, pulling open the wide door so Bert could hobble through. Behind him a torrent of passengers piled in. He stopped for a minute, confused, until his brothers caught up with him. Ed, capable as usual, took the lead.

"We'll have to check in with the airlines people over at the counter," his older brother said. He reached into his coat pocket, pulled out three envelopes containing the tickets and handed them to a smiling, efficient girl.

"Three for Salt Lake City," she said. "Your plane is at Gate One, out through that door. Have a nice trip. The porter will load your luggage."

Out through the door leading to the flight runway, Bert could see a massive, glittering plane.

"Boy, just look at the size of that plane!" Howard said to him, his freckled face rapt with wonder.

At the foot of a flight of steps leading up to the plane door, an efficient stewardess checked off their names, and the three boys climbed aboard.

"We're the first on, so we get the choice of seats," Bert said to his brothers. "Let's sit in the back here, so we can look out and not have the wing in the way." They settled themselves comfortably in the deep chairs, Ed and Bert on one side of the aisle; Howard, with his nose pressed against the glass, in one of two seats on the opposite side. Other passengers, including the dark-haired stranger, filed aboard, and a crewman swung shut the door.

There was a faint, squealing noise as the pilot warmed up the motors, and then a loud, drumming roar as first one motor and then the other sprang to life. The plane slowly taxied out to the end of the runway and swung round. The roar grew louder, and the plane seemed to strain against the brakes that kept it from taking off.

Bert's eyes widened with wonder and a little apprehension. His older brother patted him reassuringly on the shoulder.

"He's just making sure that the motors are okay before he takes off," Ed shouted into his brother's ear. "Now, let's fasten our safety belts."

All three boys carefully tightened the canvas straps around their waists. As they did so, the plane skimmed forward and left the ground with a final roar and a smooth motion that dropped Bert's heart into his stomach. As he peered out the window, he could see the ground dropping away. In a moment Boston was a doll-house city, glittering in the sun and growing smaller every second.

"You can unfasten your seat belts now," the hostess said to Bert, leaning over his shoulder. "Also, you can walk around if you want to."

Bert lifted himself up and hobbled forward to a seat just in front of the mammoth airplane wing. Absorbed in the pattern of scenery below—farms, rivers, tiny villages—he scarcely noticed that the dark young stranger was also out of his seat and moving around. A moment later the stranger sat down beside him.

"Beautiful, isn't it?" the stranger said to him. Bert nodded agreement.

"Did I hear you say you were going to Salt Lake City?" continued the stranger.

"That's right," said Bert. "You going there too?"

"That's right," said the stranger. "My name's Alan Wallace. My dad's a miner out there. I was in school just outside of Boston, but I—I got tired of it, and I'm going back home to stay. What're you going to do in Utah?"

"Ski, of course," responded Bert. "And we're going out there to look for an old mine—"

He caught himself as Alan leaned forward in his chair and said, "An old mine? Where in Utah is this old mine?"

As Bert was about to reply, he somehow sensed that Ed was standing in the aisle beside his chair and that of the stranger's. He glanced up just in time to catch a warning frown and a barely perceptible shake of the head from his older brother.

"Well, it doesn't matter much where it is," he said quickly. "I guess there are lots of old mines around Utah, aren't there? Anyway, I want you to meet my older brother, Ed Walton. I'm Bert, and that's my younger brother, Howard, sitting back there in the other chair."

Wallace acknowledged the introductions with a grudging nod and then excused himself. "I think I'll take a nap," he explained. "This flight is old stuff to me, and I'm a little tired."

As Alan moved to a seat a little farther ahead, Ed sat down in his place. "Boy, you don't want to talk to strangers about that mine," he said earnestly. "You don't know who this Wallace lad is—maybe he knows something we don't."

"Ah, you're crazy, Ed," Bert said gaily. "How would a stranger know or care about our mine?"

"Just the same, don't talk about it," Ed warned his brother. "And keep that map right in your watch pocket."

As the miles sped by, the frequent landings and take-offs began to lose their fascination, and the dull, thrumming roar of the motors made Bert sleepier and sleepier. At last he dozed, but a particularly rough bit of air woke him again, and he opened his eyes to see Alan drop into the seat beside him.

"Got the time?" Alan inquired.

Bert reached for the ancient turnip of a watch his father had given him long ago. As he sleepily pulled it out, the map came with it and dropped to the floor. Before he could reach forward to retrieve it, Alan had pounced upon the yellowed slip of paper. It had been badly folded and one corner was bent back. Visible on that corner was the word "Sunmount."

"Here it is," said Alan, his eyes flicking from the map to Bert and back again. "And here we are at Omaha. We've got an hour's stopover here while they refuel the plane. By the way, I know Omaha pretty well. I've got to ride downtown a minute to see a man. How about coming with me?"

Though Bert felt a twinge of unwillingness, he followed Alan as the latter hailed a cab and they sped down into the center of Omaha. At the doors of a big hotel, the cab swung in to the curb.

"Excuse me a minute while I go see this friend of mine," Alan said to Bert as they walked into the bustling lobby. "You just sit down in the corner and I'll be right back." He gave a farewell wave of the hand as he vanished behind some potted palms, and Bert absorbed himself in the shifting panorama of guests strolling through the lobby. Not until some minutes had passed did he happen to look up at the mammoth clock over the hotel desk. He realized with a shock that only fifteen minutes remained before departure time—and Alan was nowhere in sight.

"Well, I hate to do it, but I've got to make that plane," he said to himself. "I'll just have to get a cab back by myself." But out in front of the hotel there was not a cab in sight. Desperate, Bert finally appealed to the uniformed doorman.

"Why, bud, you ain't got a chance," the doorman drawled, shifting a toothpick from one side of his mouth to the other. "There's a big parade on, and no cab can get through the streets downtown until the parade's finished."

"But I've got to make that plane!" Bert wailed, thoroughly alive at last to his predicament. "My brothers are on it, and we're all going to Salt Lake City."

"Well, nuthin' can get through but a police car," observed the doorman. "In fact, there's one right now." He gestured toward the street, and Bert could see a sedan with "Police" painted on its sides moving slowly toward them. He acted instinctively. He limped to the center of the street as fast as he could and held up one hand just like a traffic policeman. The sedan squealed to a stop, and its uniformed driver looked out quizzically.

"I'm in trouble," Bert blurted out. "I've just got to get to the airport!"

As he explained his predicament, the words tumbling

over one another, the half-frown on the policeman's face gave way slowly to a sympathetic grin.

"Why, boy, I guess this *is* an emergency," observed the policeman, pushing back his visored cap to scratch his head. "It's against the rules, but I guess I can explain it to the sergeant. So hop in."

As the police sedan slid into high gear, the patrolman flicked a switch, and a low, muttering sound under the hood grew to the scream of a siren. The car dropped down-hill toward the parading masses on a cross street. Bert could see faces turned toward the car from both sides of the street. He could hear the shrill whistles of traffic policemen and then masses of people halted as the car knifed through the parade and came out again on quieter streets.

Pulling his watch from his pocket, he frantically glanced at the time. Five minutes to two and the plane left at two o'clock! The patrolman nodded reassuringly. "We'll make it," he said and pushed the accelerator to the floor.

Swerving, lurching, narrowly missing other cars, the sedan swept forward and with a squeal swung round the corner and in front of the terminal building just as the clock in the lobby registered two. A voice on the loudspeaker was plaintively squawking, "Mr. Bert Walton, please."

With a hasty word of thanks, Bert hurried out through the doors to the side of the plane, where his two worried brothers were solemnly conferring. A grin lit their faces as he hobbled up to them, and then all three hastened on board ship.

"But what happened?" the other boys demanded.

"Ask *him,*" Bert said angrily, gesturing toward Alan, who had half risen from his seat. At the sound of the words, Alan walked rapidly back toward Bert.

"Good grief!" he said. "I was half crazy with worry. It took me longer than I'd expected, and when I came downstairs again, there was such a crowd in the lobby and it was so late I figured you'd already taken the plane. So I sneaked across through the parade before the police could stop me and took a cab on the other side. Gosh, I'm sorry about this!"

Bert's face, at first dark with suspicion, took on a forgiving expression as Alan made his convincing explanation, but Ed, sitting beside him, still looked doubtfully at the glib young stranger.

"That's all right," said Bert. "I see now what's happened. We were both to blame."

The roar of the motors cut off their conversation and, as

the plane sped forward in its take-off, Alan settled himself in a seat far ahead of the brothers.

As he leaned toward his brother, cupping his left ear to hear above the roar of the motors, he heard Ed say, "If he was so worried about you, why didn't he say something to us when he got aboard the plane? He just sat down and didn't say a word, but he was smiling to himself. We'd better keep our eye on that fellow."

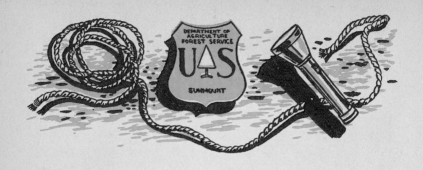

4   *Boulders in the Canyon*

In the gathering dusk the plane slid forward over another range of snow-capped mountains—and there, in the wide valley, were the lights of Salt Lake City.

"Fasten seat belts," commanded the blinking sign in the front of the cabin, and the boys obeyed as the ship dropped steadily down toward the growing brightness of the city.

"We're here," Bert said to his brothers. His voice sounded strange to him, and there was a ringing in his ears caused by the change from high altitude to ground level. He closed his mouth, swallowed, and could hear the faint pop as his ears adjusted themselves. "We're here," he repeated. "Wonder if anybody will meet us."

"Well, Dad said he had asked Mr. Wilson, a lawyer, to come out," contributed Howard. "But I don't see many people waiting out there."

The plane rolled to a stop, a wheeled staircase was pushed out from the terminal building, and a mechanic in overalls opened the door from the outside. The three boys, blinking a little, moved down the steps and toward the terminal. Nobody came forward to greet them, and they halted indecisively just as the loudspeaker boomed out a message.

"Will the three Walton boys please report to the information desk? Will the three Walton boys please report to the information desk?"

At the desk a pleasant young man looked up from his papers and said, "If you're the Walton boys, I have a message for you. Mr. Wilson phoned out and said he will be unable to meet you because of an emergency law case. But there will be a Mr. Holliday, a Mr. Muldrow Holliday, the ranger from Sunmount, arriving in a few minutes. He will take you up the mountain."

The relief on Bert's face was mirrored by that of his brothers. As he turned away from the counter, however, his expression changed quickly. "Look," he said in an undertone, nudging Ed. "Do you see what I see?"

Outside, half visible in the lights and shadows of the airport apron, stood Alan Wallace, busily engaged in conversation with a gray-haired, grim-faced, elderly man, on whose face the stiff bristles of an unshorn beard stood out. It was a furtive conversation, and now and then the two men glanced toward the interior of the terminal.

"I still say there's something funny going on here," mused Ed. "First the way Alan cross-examined you about the mine, then that business of getting you almost lost in downtown Omaha."

"Oh, you're too suspicious," broke in Howard as a grin spread across his freckled face. "I think you're imagining things. What do you think, Bert?"

"I don't really know," said Bert. "I'm not sure which of you is right."

Before he could explain his reasoning, a hand fell on his shoulder and a hearty voice said. "I'm sure you must be the Walton boys. If you are, I've got a ride for you."

The boys swung around and looked up into the bronzed face of Muldrow Holliday. He was dressed in the green uniform of the United States Forest Service, and an embroidered green pine tree, insigne of his work, stood out prominently on his left sleeve. He was a tall man, taller than any of the boys, and his quiet speech inspired confidence.

"We'll have to be careful going up the canyon tonight," he said as he strolled with the boys toward the baggage counter. "We had a big storm up here yesterday, and some of the snow is still avalanching. I've closed the gates at both ends of the canyon, and only the people who live up there have keys to the locks."

"You mean it's really so dangerous?" Bert inquired.

"Yup," said Holliday, "it's not like the East, where the trees keep the snow from sliding. Out here an avalanche can sweep away a whole town; in fact, it swept away the whole town of Sunmount some years ago, and there's never been a real settlement there since. But let's get the baggage and talk about that later."

It took a little time to collect the carefully strapped skis, the packs, and the bags; but at last the boys staggered out through the door, following Holliday. As they stepped into the crisp, cold air, a battered jalopy rattled past them, and they caught a glimpse of Alan Wallace and the man, their faces turned away from them.

"A funny pair," Holliday observed. "Don't know how they make a living. The old man never seems to have any money, but still he managed to send the boy away to school. Used to be talk that they had a secret gold mine somewhere up in the hills, but nobody was ever able to prove anything. They're stubborn, though—keep going off into avalanche areas, even though I warn 'em. Someday they may regret it."

As he talked, he loaded the skis onto a convenient rack atop his sedan, unlocked the trunk, and deftly swung the packs and bags inside. The boys climbed in, Holliday stepped on the starter, and with a muffled roar they swept out of the airport grounds and up toward the mountains that glittered palely in the moonlight.

The car began to swing up from the plain and toward the shadowy entrance to a canyon overhung by cliffs and glittering slopes of snow. From somewhere ahead came a faint, rumbling sound.

"Avalanche," said Holliday, "but it's far off in the hills."

A faint beam flickered ahead of them, a car coming their way. As they moved uphill, the lights finally burst around the corner. The road was icy, and the tires on Holliday's car hissed and sang as he carefully maneuvered it. Now the lights were coming closer, closer.

"Jumping Jupiter!" burst from Holliday's lips. He gave a mighty heave at the steering wheel. The car lurched, slid, and rocked. It skidded along the shoulder of the road and then skated from side to side as the other auto faded out of sight.

"Mighty funny he should skid right there," said Holliday thoughtfully. "That's a straight piece of road, and I've never had any trouble on it. Of course, when you've got an old jalopy like Tom Wallace's—"

"Wallace?" broke in Bert. "Is that Alan's father?"

"That's right," said Holliday. "That's exactly right."

From the back seat came Ed's quiet voice. "Well, now I wonder—I wonder more than ever."

Holliday slowed down as Ed spoke. In the headlights' beam Bert could see a massive gate, six feet high.

"That's the canyon gate," said Holliday. "Wonder if one of you boys would get out and open it. Maybe two would be better—it's hard to push."

"I'll go," said Bert. "It may do my ankle good."

"And so will I," added Ed. "I don't want you to slip and sprain it again."

The two boys stepped out gingerly. The pavement beneath their feet was a glaze of ice, treacherous to walk on with city shoes.

"Be careful," called Holliday. "It's usually very icy down here. You don't hit snow until you get higher up."

In the bright moonlight Bert could see the canyon walls seeming to hang over his head. High up there was the glitter of ice in the gullies and then, above it, reflecting the light like a million stars, the gleam of snow.

"Look at that!" he said to Ed, who had one hand under his elbow to support him. "Look at that! Real mountains and real snow. Boy, what a time we're going to have out here!"

The gate was just ahead of him. He fumbled in his right trouser pocket for the key to the padlock, which hung massively through an immense hasp and effectively closed off the canyon to intruders. The intense cold had frozen the lock, and it took Bert a minute or two before he could wiggle the key enough to make it turn in the lock. There was a faint click, and the padlock swung open.

"Works awfully hard," he observed to Ed. He puffed a little with the unaccustomed exertion. At the side of the gate a painted sign said: "Avalanche Canyon: 5,200 feet above sea level."

"Look how high we are—higher than the top of our mountain back home. Now—together—shove!"

The gate gave way reluctantly, but above the noise of its squeaky hinges was a new, strange noise—a grating, rumbling noise.

"Look out!" shouted Ed. Bert stopped in his forward

movement. As he did, the rumble increased to a roar. His brother dived backward with him, and the two boys slid together down the pavement.

As Ed untangled himself, he looked back toward the far side of the gate. There, just an inch or two from the point where he had stood, lay a huge boulder and a tangle of smaller rocks.

"Enough to kill a man," said Holliday grimly. "That's one of those boulder slides I was telling you about. You just missed by inches. And if it hadn't been for your brother here—"

Bert smiled gratefully at Ed as he rose to his feet. He saw Holliday standing by the edge of the gate, fingering something. He walked back to the gate.

Holliday turned a dark face toward him. "There's dirty work here," said the ranger. "See this piece of rope tied onto the gate? Well, I don't dare go up on that boulder slide at night, but it's just as plain as day to me. Somebody hooked a rope onto a loose boulder so that whenever the gate was pushed open, the whole pile would come down."

Sportsmen Don't Complain

"If this isn't paradise, it's the next thing to it."

The sound of Ed's voice roused Bert from a deep and dreamless sleep. As he struggled up and out of the covers, bright sunlight flashed into his eyes, and through frosty windowpanes he could see outside the Utah of the posters and magazine ads.

"Let's go!" he yelled at Howard, whose blond head was barely visible, buried as it was beneath a mound of covers. His younger brother sat up abruptly, rubbed his eyes, and then let out a whoop as he saw the snow outside.

The tiny bunkroom, with its three beds and its paneled walls, was scarcely big enough for the energetic Waltons as they hurried into their long underwear, slipped on their tapered ski trousers, hustled into their flannel shirts, and gave their faces a lick and a promise with soap and water.

"Last one down's a dope!" called Bert as he sprinted out the door. He was moving so fast that he almost collided with a little blond girl in a blue ski suit. "Oh, beg pardon—" he started to say and stepped back hastily, just in time to carom off another girl a few paces ahead of him. The red of Bert's hair was matched by the dusky color of his face and neck as he stepped aside to let the girl go by. By the time he reached the table, his color was normal again. He had just sat down when the same two girls sat down beside him.

"If you aren't still in such a hurry," the blond girl of his hallway encounter said sweetly, "we'd like to join you, since we've been eating at this table all week."

Bert gulped, and blushed again. "Why, why sure."

"My name's Mary Sue Hargreaves," said the blond girl, "and this is Betty Brower. And your name?"

"Bert Walton," he supplied quickly. "These"—indicating his brothers, who had just seated themselves—"are my two brothers, Ed and Howard. We're out from New England for some deep snow skiing."

"Well, you've picked the right place," said Mary Sue. "And this is the right day. There's a *slalom* race for the guests today, and, of course, all of you will want to enter."

Bert looked inquiringly at his two brothers, who nodded.

"Why, sure," he said. "But we'll probably fall all the way down the hill. We're new at this western skiing. Back home everything is hard-packed snow."

"Well, in *slalom* it's pretty nearly the same out here," observed Mary Sue. "They keep the course well-tramped. Sometimes a gate may get a little rutted, but in general it's just about the same as in the East."

As the girls rose from the table, Bert and his brothers rose, too, and strolled into the living room. They wore their ski boots, but the laces were tied loosely so that they could walk in comfort. A stout, gray-haired man in a tweed suit was sitting in the corner, glancing at the morning's newspaper. He looked up as they entered and then came forward with his right hand extended.

"I'm Mr. Wilson," he greeted the brothers. "Sorry I missed you last night."

"That's not all you missed," replied Bert, shaking hands and introducing his brothers. He went on to tell the lawyer about their adventures in the canyon—the car that nearly forced them off the road, the boulders that nearly trapped them as they opened the gate. Mr. Wilson's ruddy face darkened, but he held up a hand in warning as Bert began to express his suspicion of the Wallaces.

"Better not express your suspicions until you have more proof," he warned the boys. "There are a lot of odd ducks around these hills, and you can't be sure that the Wallaces were responsible.

"But I want you to watch your step, nevertheless. I am pretty sure that your Uncle John's missing gold mine does exist somewhere in this area; there has been enough talk of such a mine so that I'm inclined to believe it. However, we'll have to find some records to prove it. And, so far as I know, all the mining records for this section of Utah were lost when the avalanche of 1902 wiped out Sunmount."

"Then our best bet right now is to do a little skiing and a lot of thinking until we get things straight in our minds," Ed remarked, throwing an arm over Bert's shoulder.

"That's right," said Mr. Wilson, "and I'll be keeping an eye on you. I'll be up every other day or so, and if I acquire any more information about the mine, I'll let you know immediately."

Five minutes later the three Waltons were sliding smoothly downhill to the little chalet they had seen from their bunkroom window. Beside it gaily painted steel chairs hung from a steel cable.

"That's the first chair lift I've ever seen in operation,"

Bert said with awe. "Now all we have to do is to find out how we get on it."

The three boys slid up to a ticket window, put down their money, and each received in return a red tag to which a wire was attached. They tied the wires to their shirts and skied onto the platform where passengers were boarding the lift. At the far end a figure in green was bent over a huge blackboard.

"That's Mr. Holliday," said Howard. "Bet a dollar."

As he spoke, the figure turned. It was Holliday. A grin split his tanned face, and he walked quickly over to the boys.

"Glad to see you," he said. "You'll have fun today."

"But how about what happened last night?" Bert inquired curiously.

"I'm still working on that," said Holliday quickly. "I haven't got a clue as yet. The Wallaces insist they didn't come up the canyon until after we did, and they claim not to know anything about that jalopy that nearly skidded into us. So we'll just have to let things ride awhile. In the meantime, do you know how to ride this lift or where to go when you get to the top?"

"We don't know a thing," Bert answered. "Suppose you tell us."

"Well, to get on," said Holliday, "simply move into place as soon as the skier ahead of you has boarded a chair. Just stand there with your knees bent, and let the chair hit you in the back of your knees. Then sit down and keep your ski tips high when you go off the platform; otherwise you may catch them in the snow.

"As to where to go—see that blackboard? All the places I have indicated there are unsafe. There is avalanche danger. Stay away from them, and watch out for signboards indicating avalanche areas. Any place else you want to go is perfectly safe."

"Okay," said Bert, easing himself into a chair. "Here goes." The rest followed.

"Let's take a look at the *slalom*," Ed called to him and started across the hill toward the first of the collection of flags that marked the course of the race. Bert followed, a little shaky in the deep snow and grateful that he didn't have to practice high speed turns in such uncertain stuff.

"It's a tough one," he agreed with his brothers as they stood at the top. "All those combinations of flags—and, of course, if you miss one, you're out of the race."

The three boys carefully skied down alongside the *slalom* flags, being careful to observe the rule that you must not ski the actual course itself before the race. Halfway down, a bronze-faced youngster, the weight of his arms resting easily on his ski poles, greeted them with a grin. It was Alan Wallace and the grin might have been friendly or sarcastic. Bert couldn't figure which.

"This will show you Easterners something about skiing," he said to Bert. "We set tough *slaloms* here in the West."

He placed his poles in front of him, gave a spring, and started down the hill in a swirl of flying snow.

"Not for us, boys," Ed cautioned his brothers as Bert and Howard looked enviously after Alan. "We'll learn that later. For now let's just go down easy in nice, slow stem turns."

At the base of the lift all traffic had been closed off, except for competitors. A smiling, middle-aged man handed number bibs to Bert, Ed, and Howard, and they slipped them over their heads.

The thermometer needle on the lift house said that the temperature was fifteen above zero; but with the bright sun on the snow, it seemed almost like spring in New England to Bert. There was something wonderfully relaxing about this western skiing, he reflected—and woke from his reverie to hear the starter calling for "Six—number six."

"Good grief!" he said to himself. "That's me." His mouth was dry, and his eyes seemed to burn behind his green sunglasses as he moved forward into starting position and heard the old, familiar counting-off of seconds. Then he was on the way.

The first three gates were easy—a swing left, cutting close to the lower flag in the gate to straighten his run as much as possible, a swing right, and then a hairpin, two closely grouped pairs of flags which involved a sharp turn from right to left. Then the course-setter had diabolically left a long open space in which the runner had to decide whether to go straight, hoping to control his speed sufficiently for the difficult gates below, or whether to snowplow. Bert decided to be cautious. He spread the tails of his skis wide, keeping the tips together so that the skis were in a broad V and carefully slid down to the next gate.

"I'm glad I was cautious," he said to himself as he swung his body through the flush, three closely linked gates which involved three tight turns.

"Good running!" he heard a gatekeeper, watching the course and checking the runners, call out to him. Then, after two more gates, came the trickiest of all—an H where, he noted, no gatekeeper was on duty. Four red flags formed a square. Inside this square two yellow flags were placed close together. The skier had a difficult choice to make. Either he could go straight through the yellow flags, building up a burst of speed that might trap him later, or he could make two quick swings and thus cut down his speed. Bert realized he was losing time.

"The heck with it!" he said to himself and dived straight through the yellow flags. Before he knew it, he had swung down through the rest of the gates and was sliding over the finish line.

A timekeeper, watch in hand, did some quick figuring and then said to Bert, "That was good time, boy. If you didn't win, you came close."

"Came close to doing what?" a voice from the sidelines challenged. Bert swung around and looked into Alan's brown eyes.

"Came close to winning, Alan," said the timekeeper. "Unless you know something I don't."

"I do," said Alan sulkily. "He missed a gate up there on the hill."

"Missed what gate?" demanded Bert, doubling his fists.

"Missed in the H," answered Alan. "I saw you, fellow. I climbed back up to watch how you'd take it. You didn't go through the yellow flags at all."

Bert swallowed to hold back his mounting anger. He stared steadily at Alan as his rival continued, "He figured he could get away with it, I guess. There wasn't any gate-keeper there. But I saw him."

The timekeeper looked reproachfully at Bert. He shook his head and then conferred with the chief timer, who sat at a table nearby. Then he called Bert to one side and said solemnly, "Son, I don't exactly know *who's* right about this. But Alan is a local boy, and I have no reason to doubt his word. And you know yourself it's easy enough to miss a gate in the excitement of a race. So why don't you be a good sport and accept a disqualification? You're a good skier, I can see that. There'll be another race later, and I'll be up there on the hill watching you personally."

Bert nodded his head wordlessly and turned away. He started away from the crowd. As he did so, an arm reached out and stopped him.

"That's all right," said Muldrow Holliday. "Be a good sport about it. I think that Alan is laying for you, but we'll catch him and straighten out this and a lot of other things before you leave Utah."

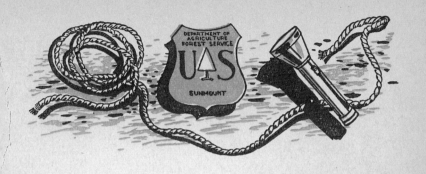

6   *Avalanche!*

The sting of being disqualified still lingered with Bert the next morning as he walked into the dining room at the chalet and looked across the familiar tables to his own spot in the corner, where Mary Sue and Betty sat. They smiled at him as he approached. When he sat down, Mary Sue leaned over and said, "Don't let it bother you, Bert. Both of us are sure you won that race, no matter what Alan says."

"Oh, I've forgotten it already," Bert said airily. "I'll just wait until next week, and then I'll win for sure."

His brothers, who were just then sitting down, heard his words. Both of them grinned and Ed winked. Bert began to feel better about the whole thing. "What's for today?" he inquired of the table in general.

"Let's go touring!" chorused the girls.

"In a car, you mean?" asked Bert, his face clouding over. He wanted to ski.

"No, silly," answered Mary Sue, "on skis. Don't you know what touring is?"

"Afraid I don't," muttered Bert, feeling a little foolish. "Suppose you tell me. I'm just a dumb New Englander."

"Why, touring is just traveling cross-country on skis," said Mary Sue. "Instead of riding the lift and skiing down, we'll ride the lift and climb up—and come back another way after lunch. You have sealskins, of course?"

"No," admitted Bert. "We always climbed on wax back East or else just sidestepped uphill."

"Well, you can't do that out here," said Mary Sue. "You'll have to buy skins in the ski shop. You strap them on the bottom of your skis, and then you can climb straight uphill. When you get to the top, just take them off, stuff them in your pack, and ski down again. Simple, isn't it?"

In the ski shop a tactful young man picked out three pairs of sealskins for them and showed the boys how to strap them on the skis. The kitchen had provided sandwiches and a Thermos bottle full of cocoa, and fifteen minutes after breakfast the three boys and two girls were reading the blackboard at the foot of the ski lift.

"Only places closed are Catamount Canyon and the Plummet Trail," said Ed after carefully looking at the board. "Apparently Blizzard Basin was closed on account of avalanche danger, but somebody has rubbed that name out."

"Oh, Blizzard Basin is the best of all," said Betty, breaking in. "Let's go there! I know the way."

The lift swiftly carried them up to a flat spot halfway up the mountain. Over their heads the sky was an unbelievable shade of blue, and the sun shone brightly, but a breeze stirred the snow. Off to their right a "closed" sign warned skiers away from Catamount Canyon. But the trail to Blizzard Basin, straight ahead, was unmarked by skis, and no warning sign was visible, only a trampled-down place where some skier had turned around, beating down the snow.

"I guess it's time to put on skins," said Bert, looking at his older brother for confirmation. Ed nodded in agreement. Howard had already taken off his skis—and, to his surprise, sank waistdeep in the soft snow.

"I forgot to warn you," Betty said, laughing, "but unless this snow is packed, you'll do better to stand on one ski while you're taking the other off. That is, unless you want to sink right through to China."

Howard ruefully agreed with her as he climbed out of
the hole he had made and balanced himself on his left ski
while he took the sealskins from his pack.

"That's our route," Betty said. Bert swung left and began
working up through a series of timbered glades and open
spaces. It was getting hotter as they climbed, and the snow
was losing some of its powdery consistency and becoming
slightly sticky.

Zigzagging across the slope, the party soon reached the
open top of the mountain. From the bare rocks where the
snow had melted, they looked out across a sea of mountains
to the plain of the Great Salt Lake. Their skis, stuck upright
in the snow, framed a spectacular panorama.

"Who'd ever have thought we'd get to see something like
this!" said Howard. His freckled face was redder than
ever. "Sunshine, snow, and wonderful scenery—"

"Chow!" Bert called to Ed and the girls, who had
strolled over to the other side of the peak and were busy
chatting among themselves about what they could see down
in the valley.

Lunch had never tasted so good. The chef had put up
every kind of sandwich a youngster would like; the cocoa

was steaming hot, so warm that it burned Bert's hands when he poured it into the aluminum cap of the Thermos bottle and tried to drink some. There were pickles, and even a few pieces of hard candy.

"Ah, luxury!" sighed Howard, leaning back against a boulder as if it were an overstuffed chair. "Let's sleep."

Some time later—it may have been an hour, it may have been two—Bert woke from his sleep. The sun had dropped perceptibly over the edge of Baldy Mountain. The others were still sound asleep.

"Hey!" he said to them, shaking one after the other, "time to go. We want to have some fun on the way down."

The various members of the party awoke reluctantly, and it took longer than Bert had expected to get organized.

"Which way down, girls?" inquired Bert, removing his glasses to polish them before the trip. Mary Sue's golden hair reflected the sinking sun as she pointed down into an area perhaps half a mile away from the slopes up which they had climbed.

"That's the most fun," she said. "Steep slopes, so you can swing more easily. Lots of open country. Sometimes it's avalanche country, but according to the blackboard it's safe today. Let's go."

Straight ahead of them a ridge sloped down gently and then ran out onto a little plateau. Bert dug in his poles, dove over the edge, and swept down to the plateau without making a turn. The first fifteen feet of running showed him that he could not lean forward in the same deep, crouching position he was accustomed to using for downhill and *slalom* on packed slopes or trails. When he did so, his ski tips began to bury themselves. Instead he had to preserve the same deep knee bend, but at the same time he had to lean back a little so that the ski tips planed atop the snow.

As he coasted to a stop on the plateau, he looked back and saw that Ed was learning the lesson the hard way. He was wallowing in the snow halfway up the hill while the others slid by him.

"I think I've got the secret, Ed," Bert confided to his brother. "Just lean back a little. There's so much resistance in this snow that you'll have to make your body swing much more powerfully than we do back East. Here, let me try."

He dived off the edge of the plateau. As his skis gained speed, he began the counterswing, and then smoothly carved himself a wide, spraying turn in the snow. Here in the shade it was powdery again. But below, where the sun had been blasting down, he reminded himself he must be more cautious. He completed another turn and then swung to a stop, using all the power, discipline and knowledge at his command. The turn came around perfectly.

"That does it!" he said. "Let's run down through!"

From that point on it was pure bliss. His skis responded to every movement. His turns came around perfectly. He moved through the fluffy snow as if he had wings. Open glades gave way to timbered areas where he made short, sharp turns through the narrow space between the ponderosa pine. Timbered areas, in turn, gave way to what must in summer be great meadows where the sheep could graze. Finally he stopped at a point where the ground dropped away in the final plunge to the valley floor.

Far behind him came the others, little dots silhouetted against the snow, swinging in linked turns, coming closer, crossing each other's tracks. He could catch the flying blond hair of Mary Sue, and the flaming red parka worn by Betty. He could see Ed, skiing as steadily as a rock, and little Howard, with dash and precision. Finally all of them swung to a stop beside him, breathless but grinning with the sheer joy of a run well made. To either side of the final schuss, the final slope to the valley, the pine trees crowded in, but an area at least a quarter mile wide was clear of trees—and steep—steeper than anything Bert had ever seen except the dizzy headwall of Tuckerman's Ravine, back on Mt. Washington in New Hampshire. The hill seemed to bulge out in the middle.

"Howie, why don't you go first?" asked Bert. "I'll follow you, and the others can pick their own track behind me."

"Okay," Howard replied. "Here goes nothing!"

He leaned forward against his poles and shoved off into space. Bert let a second elapse and then followed him. Bobbing and weaving, they traced a pattern on the snow and then plunged over the bulge. Howard was scarcely fifteen feet ahead and just starting a new turn when Bert felt a strange movement beneath his skis. Involuntarily he looked down.

The snow seemed to be separating. It seemed to be splitting under the skis, sliding away—*an avalanche!*

"Howie!" he yelled and flung himself forward on his skis. He hit his younger brother a football tackle's blow and flung him out into the widely spaced trees. Behind him, in the open area, a slow rumbling rose to a roar. As Bert pulled himself to his skis, he could see a cloud of snow rising from the valley floor; and then, as it cleared away, the track of an avalanche. It had swept halfway across the valley.

"If it hadn't been for you, I'd be in the middle of that slide," Howard said breathlessly to his brother.

"Yeah," said Bert, "but did the others miss it?" He swung himself around and looked up through the trees. Mingled with the shadows were skiers: One . . . two . . . three. . . . He sighed with relief. Everybody accounted for.

"You all right?" the cry came down to him. He raised one hand and waved his ski pole as a rallying signal. Mary Sue and Betty, white-faced and trembling, were the first to join him.

Then came Ed, and his first question was, "What happened? I thought this hill was safe to ski today."

"So did I," Bert answered grimly. "And it doesn't occur to me that Mr. Holliday could be so careless. There's something mighty peculiar about this. Let's go on down and see if we can find out what went wrong or who wanted something to go wrong."

7   *Who Is to Blame?*

The nonchalant grin which served as Bert's trademark was replaced by a grimly serious expression as he pointed his skis down through the open forest, heading for the summit of the chair lift.

"Let's take it easy," he called back as he dropped lower and lower through the trees, using his ski pole as a pivoting point for a series of precise, lifted stem turns. Ed, calm and thoughtful as always, was just behind him. "Good old Ed," mused Bert. "He doesn't need to be told."

"What, no more racing?" The voice of Howard came down to him. He glanced back to see his younger brother, his face pale beneath his freckles, moving shakily down in the track of the two older boys. It had been a shock for Howard, coming so close to death, and Bert could see that his usually carefree young brother was wobbly on his skis.

"Well," he thought to himself, "maybe it's safe to take it straight the rest of the way down. Might be easier for Howard than making all these turns." Ahead of him he could see a straight path through the trees to the level floor of the basin.

"Okay," he called, "let's go!" The wind hummed in his ears. The purplish tree trunks clicked by like telegraph poles seen from the windows of a train. Then he had left the last of the trees behind and was gliding out over the open, sunny basin floor. He let his skis coast until they had no more momentum. As he slowed down, the others overtook him. They were smiling again; the shock had worn off.

A little to their left the snow was piled in great ridges and hummocks—the fan of the avalanche. Along its outer edge a figure on skis was moving, half-hidden by the wall of snow. A second later Bert saw who it was.

"Mr. Holliday!" he called. The ranger, still some distance away, raised a pole in greeting and began to glide toward them in a smooth, swinging cross-country step. Bert had to admire his speed and efficiency in skiing on the level.

The ranger's face, usually lit by a warm smile, was frozen in forbidding lines, but a little relief was visible, too.

"I was beginning to wonder if I'd have to call out the rescue parties," Holliday greeted them. "I saw the lot of you skiing down the top of the hill, and then the avalanche began, and I didn't quite know what had happened."

"Oh, Bert saved me," broke in Howard eagerly. "He shoved me off to one side just as the avalanche broke away. The girls and Ed were farther up the hill. We're all right, Mr. Holliday. Don't worry."

"I'm not worrying," the ranger said slowly, "but maybe you ought to be. Didn't you know that this hillside had been closed because of avalanche danger?"

"Closed?" asked Bert, and there was sincerity in his voice. "But the Blizzard Basin trail wasn't listed as closed on the blackboard. It had been, but somebody rubbed out the name."

"I'm afraid you'll have to prove that to me," said Holliday, doubtfully. His tanned face still was solemn. "Anyway there was a warning sign at the top. I put it up myself."

"But where?" asked Bert. He was beginning to feel a little frantic. Had there really been a warning sign, and had he missed it?

"Boys," said the ranger, a little doubt in his own voice, "I want to believe you. I know all sorts of strange things have been happening to you—starting with the accident we almost had on the highway, and then the pile of boulders that came down at the gate—but this is a little too pat. I can't believe that anybody would deliberately try to lure you onto an avalanche slope and get you killed."

"Maybe if I tell you why we're here," Bert said stoutly, "you'd understand. Just come off to one side with me a moment while I talk to you."

The ranger skied a few paces away, and Bert quickly joined him. Then, in a lowered voice, Bert confided the story of the mysterious gold mine and his suspicions of Alan Wallace and the latter's father, Tom.

"Well, the gold mine part of the story sounds possible, though fantastic," the ranger admitted. "But I can't believe that the Wallaces would stoop to such tricks. They're cantankerous people, both of 'em, but I don't think they're unscrupulous. Let's go take a close look at the avalanche fan before we stop down by the lift to see what happened to my warning sign."

At a signal from Bert the rest of the party joined him, and they followed close behind Holliday as he moved along the edge of the avalanche.

"You see how deep this snow is piled," he said to Bert,

who nodded acknowledgment. "Well, anyone caught in it could never escape alive. You can't outski an avalanche like this, once it has started to roll. And even if you're nearby, you might conceivably be suffocated in the cloud of snow that rises as the avalanche rolls down to the valley."

"Then what saved us from suffocation?" Howard asked.

"What saved you," said the ranger, "was the fact that you were back of the crest of the hill. The avalanche cloud went straight up in the air, and it was, fortunately, so far away from you that none of the snow dust fell in your direction."

"What makes an avalanche?" inquired Ed. He always had to know all the details.

"A number of things," said the ranger, prodding at the lumpy snow with the point of his ski pole. "A heavy snow may fall over an icy crust, to which it is not bonded. The same snow may fall on grass, over which it can slide. Left alone, it will come down by itself in one to three days. But if someone ventures out on it, then—look out! Down comes the avalanche, and usually the skier comes with it."

"Brr!" shivered Howard, whose eyes grew bigger and bigger as the ranger continued his explanation. "Now I'm really scared! But what do you do if you're out on a ski tour and you *have* to cross an avalanche slope?"

"When that happens," Holliday said, "your best bet is to stay widely spaced. Perhaps two hundred yards apart. Loosen your ski bindings so you can kick off your skis if necessary. Hold your ski poles in your hands. Don't have the straps around your wrists. If an avalanche starts, throw away your poles, kick off your skis, and use a strong swimming motion to stay on top of the snow as you are carried down."

"And will that save you?" asked Bert, as wide-eyed as his younger brother.

"In all likelihood, yes," said Holliday. "But the best bet is to stay away from avalanche slopes and observe the signs. Around here we bar you for the season if you disobey the signs. I don't want to do that to you youngsters if I can help it, so let's go back and see what became of the warning sign I put up this morning."

With Bert following just behind the ranger, the party slid speedily across the floor of the basin to a point just above the lift. Holliday scratched his head as he came to a stop and began to probe with his ski pole. There was the sound of steel on wood as his tip hit something beneath the snow. He bent forward and, with mittened hands, pulled up the warning sign. "Avalanche Area," it said. "Stay Off."

"Well, I'll be darned!" burst out Bert. "That sign was right under the place where it looked as if someone had stepped around on skis. What do you bet that somebody hid it there on purpose?"

"Hid it there, or accidentally knocked it over," said Holliday.

"That sounds reasonable to me, Bert," Ed remarked.

"Well, maybe," conceded Bert. "But now let's go down to the bottom and see about that blackboard. I still insist that the name of Blizzard Basin was rubbed off."

The area along the lift was packed as solidly as an Eastern ski hill, and Holliday led the way down at a speed that made Bert's eyes water, even under the protection of thick-lensed glasses. They spun down through the "corridor," a twisting lane amid trees, and then straightened out for the long, gentle but bumpy run to the base station. By the time all of them had climbed onto the platform beside the moving chairs, Holliday was standing beside the blackboard and holding firmly to the shoulder of a ragged, bearded man with a lined, twisted face.

"You let me go, Muldrow Holliday!" the bearded man whined. "I ain't done nothing I ain't got a right to do!"

"You haven't got a right to tamper with this blackboard!" Holliday snapped back.

"What was he doing, Mr. Holliday?" Bert asked.

"Fooling with the blackboard!" Holliday said indignantly. "Look here!"

He lifted the stranger's frayed coat. The tail was smeared with chalk, and all the legends on the blackboard had been half obliterated.

"Well, I got a right to do that," the stranger repeated doggedly. "After all, I own this whole canyon, everything in it. You guv'ment men got no right to put up these ski devices or to keep me out."

"Go on," Holliday barked, giving the stranger a shove. "Get out of here. And don't let me see you fooling around this blackboard again, or I'll have the police run you in."

The stranger jammed his battered and stained felt hat over his eyes and sidled past the Walton boys, giving them a sidelong look as he passed.

"I'm rich," he muttered, "rich! And they've taken it all away from me. All but the Skeleton Mine. I've still got that, and I won't tell nobody where it is."

"Good grief!" Bert said breathlessly. "What's the matter with that fellow?"

"Oh, that's poor Willis King," Holliday said indulgently. "Poor fellow is crazy. He used to prospect up here all alone. It finally drove him out of his mind. Now he thinks he owns the whole valley, and he hates skiers. He thinks they are trespassing."

"You mean he was the one who rubbed the name of Blizzard Basin off the blackboard this morning?" asked Howard, who hated to think evil of anyone.

"Looks that way, doesn't it?" said Holliday. "And that seems to dispose of some of your suspicions, Bert."

But even after a meal, hearty enough to make anyone feel benevolent, doubt still struggled with logic in Bert's mind. Coming out of the dining room behind his brothers, he had his head bent, thinking things over. He was abruptly aroused from his reverie by a tap on the shoulder.

"You're wanted on the telephone," a bellboy said.

Bert turned toward the phone booth, and for a moment the Wallaces were forgotten. He picked up the receiver.

"Bert?" inquired a voice at the other end. "This is Mr. Wilson. I have some news for you."

"What is it?" asked Bert, his pulse tingling a little.

"I've been consulting some of the old-time mine owners and prospectors down here in the city," continued the voice, "and they have helped me to narrow down the location of your mine to two areas. It is either in Panorama Gap or else up somewhere around the old tunnel on the side of Mount Holliss."

"Gravy!" said Bert, awe in his voice. "How'd you find out?"

"I did a lot of walking around and a lot of talking," came back Mr. Wilson's voice, "and I finally located two old fellows who remembered a man resembling your Uncle John. The only trouble was that they disagreed on the location of the mine.

"Now, it's up to you to find it. Good luck, and I'll be waiting to hear from you."

With trembling fingers Bert hung up the receiver. He tried to conceal his excitement as he edged his way out of the telephone booth. His two brothers were standing at one of the large windows. Seeing Bert, they smiled and pointed.

Outside, in the pale light of a single electric bulb on the terrace, he could see thin flakes falling steadily.

"Snow!" he said to himself. And then louder, "Snow! Let's go to bed and be ready for some first-class skiing in the morning!"

8 *The Skeleton in the Mine*

In the morning the snow was still falling. It lay in deep, feathery mounds outside the terrace, and had piled halfway up the door that led outside from the waxing room. As Bert gave his skis a final polish with a waxing cork, he whistled a tuneless bar of music.

A speculative look came into Bert's eyes. "Hey," he said. Both brothers turned to look at him. "I think I'll rest awhile instead of going out right away."

Ed looked at him searchingly, a little tinge of suspicion in his eyes.

"You're not going to do anything foolish, are you?" he asked. "Such as looking for evidence against Alan?"

"That's the last thing I had in my mind," Bert said firmly. He passed his hand over his hair, anchoring the red cowlick firmly in place.

"Okay," chorused his brothers, lifting their skis to their shoulders. "See you later." The wide, brass-studded door swung open, admitting a whiff of cold air and a flurry of snow, and then they were gone. Bert ran a speculative hand over the glittering finish on his skis and tightened his lips resolutely as he carefully lifted the skis from the waxing table, stood them on end in a locker, and shut the locker door tightly.

He went up the stairs two at a time and strolled whistling into the living room. It was empty, except for a bellboy sitting on a bench in the corner.

"Uh, nice day, isn't it?" he said. The bellboy nodded agreement.

"You been around here long?" Again the bellboy nodded. Bert took a grip on himself and then burst out with the question he had been holding back.

"Do you know an old prospector named Willis King?"

"Oh, the crazy old fellow? Sure. I know him."

"Where does he hang out during the day? Around the lift, or at his cabin?"

"Oh, neither place," said the bellboy, shifting his weight on the hard bench. "He's generally out around the kitchen door. He panhandles all his meals here. Funny old guy.

Claims to own all this valley. He's always talking about some mine with a skeleton in it."

"Then you don't believe what he says?" asked Bert, trying to keep the impatience out of his voice.

"Ah, no," said the bellboy. "He's crazy as a bedbug. But he's fun to talk to."

"Well, I guess I'll be getting on," said Bert, jamming both hands into his pockets and whistling as he walked away. He strolled out through the door to the terrace, then took his hands from his pockets and walked purposefully around to the kitchen door. Just inside, half hidden by the steam from the pots and pans, Willis King was sitting in a battered chair. He was talking loudly, but the grinning cook and dishwasher were paying absolutely no attention.

"Why," he said, flicking his eyes toward Bert, who let himself carefully in through the door, "I mind the days when I went down to Salt Lake with a bag o' gold dust in my hip pocket—a thousand dollar worth—and I spent it all, ever' cent of it, on the biggest party you ever did see!"

Bert seated himself on an upturned barrel, rested his chin in his hands, and listened intently to the cracked voice of the old prospector.

Suddenly the prospector broke off and fixed his beady

eyes on Bert. A grimace passed across his face, and for a moment Bert thought he was going to break down and cry.

"But you don't believe me," he half-blubbered, passing a bony wrist across his eyes. "Nobody believes me. Everybody laughs at me!"

"I don't laugh at you," Bert said sympathetically. "I believe you, Mr. King."

The mistrust on King's face vanished and was replaced by a look of doglike devotion. He leaned forward and stared into Bert's face. "You do?" he asked. "And you believe I'm rich?"

"Of course you're rich," Bert answered. In the back of his mind, he felt a twinge of conscience at this deception, but he had reasoned it out: if he made the prospector feel happy, it would be doing no harm. He might even be doing himself some good.

"Of course you're rich," he repeated earnestly. "I've heard about the Skeleton Mine, you know. That's where your gold comes from, doesn't it?"

"Come closer, boy," the prospector whispered to him. Bert hitched up his barrel. His heart began to pound, and he could feel its thump-thump-thump against his chest.

"You're the first person's been kind to me in twenty

years," whispered the prospector, "so I'm going to let you in on a secret. I'm going to tell you where the Skeleton Mine is—and, what's more, I'm going to take you there!" He shifted his chair and hitched it back against the wall. He buttoned the collar of his hickory shirt, pushed open the door, and beckoned to Bert with one bony finger.

For a moment Bert felt a twinge of hesitancy and an urge to refuse. He debated desperately whether to give some signal to the cook and dishwasher. But, as his father had said long ago, "Bert is never one to refuse a dare." He buttoned his jacket and stepped out behind the prospector.

It seemed to Bert that they had been plodding endlessly upward. Ahead of him dimly visible through the swirling snow, he could see the bent figure of Willis King. Though they were climbing through country that seemed to be completely untracked, Bert found firm footing for his ski boots, evidence that a well-beaten path existed there.

In the shelter of a clump of spruce he pushed forward to Willis King's side. The prospector lifted one ear flap of his checkered cap as Bert shouted into his ear, "Where are we? Where are we going?"

"All I'll say is we're near Pan'rama Gap, boy," came back

the reply, faint against the noise of a gathering wind.

Ahead loomed another cluster of spruce trees—small ones this time, a solid barrier. Willis King pushed in among the trees. Bert took a deep breath and plunged after him. The branches seemed to be trying to hold him back. The needles stung as they whipped against his averted face.

Suddenly, he pushed up against Willis King and came to an abrupt stop. In front of him was a wall of rock, and in the wall was a great door with iron strips running across its width. Willis King put one finger to the side of his nose, assumed a sly expression, and said to Bert, "Now, boy, you're going to see something I've never showed any other man. You're going to see the Skeleton Mine, where I get my gold."

The door creaked as the prospector drew back a bolt and pushed inward. A musty odor swept out. Bert drew a deep breath and stepped inside. There was the scratch of a match being struck on stone, and then a tiny candle began to shed a faint glow. In its beam Bert could see the rock walls glistening overhead. A rusty pick and shovel stood against one wall, damp from the moisture of underground springs. A little way back in the tunnel, where darkness began, he could see a heap of rock. Willis King seated himself on this rock pile, pulled out a pipe, lit it, and began to suck contentedly. Bert noted with a shock that King had failed to put any tobacco into the pipe.

"This is it, boy," King said expansively. "This is the Skeleton Mine."

"But why the name?" Bert asked curiously. "Why the Skeleton Mine?"

"I don't know's I ought to tell you," the prospector said slowly. "Might frighten you. But I guess I will, anyway. Years ago, when Sunmount was a real, thrivin' city, some Eastern feller—I disremember his name—come out here prospectin'. He wasn't a real prospector, you might say. He had money, and he hired men to prospect for him.

"One of those fellers came up here and dug this tunnel. I saw him—I watched him—from over on Mount Adams. This here Eastern feller come up once to see how he was doin'. He took some samples and went away, and never come back again. And then one day, when I was moseyin' around, I noticed that nobody was workin' up here. I peeked in, and I saw what happened. The walls had caved in on that there feller. I tried to dig him out, but I couldn't get down that deep in the rock. So I guess he's still underneath where I'm sittin'."

His eyes glittered as he told his story, and Bert felt a sudden shudder. He carefully controlled the quiver in his voice as he hunched forward from his seat on the doorsill of the tunnel and asked, "Do you know where in the East this man you're talking about came from?"

The prospector rubbed one wrinkled hand over his gray bristle of beard before answering.

"I disremember exactly," he finally replied. "But I think it was some little town in New England."

Bert felt his heart jump. New England! Could this be Uncle John's mine? He tried to appear nonchalant as he reached over and hefted a lump of gleaming stone. On its surface he could see the glitter of tiny particles of—gold?

"None of that, boy!" the prospector gruffly interrupted. "This is *my* gold. Don't want strangers takin' it away."

Bert forced a grin and leaned back casually. "I'm sorry," he apologized. "Didn't mean to be inquisitive."

"That's all right," the prospector said gruffly. "Just don't like people pryin' around too much." His eyes seemed to glitter and then to fade, in the light of the candle. Bert stole a glance at the rough wooden stool where the candle was burning.

"Mind if I look around a little more?" he asked. The

prospector nodded assent. Bert rose carefully, strolled toward the table, leaned over as if to look at the pick and shovel that stood alongside, and then took a step forward. He felt his right foot catch the leg of the table, and it went over with a crash. The candle was snuffed out, and in the darkness he could hear the prospector muttering.

"Dawgone clumsy!" Willis King said. Bert fumbled frantically on the floor of the tunnel. His finger touched something rough. It was the piece of rock he had been examining. He slipped it inside his shirt while apologizing profusely. He swung away as the prospector scratched another match, righted the table, and lit the candle again.

"Hadn't we better be going?" asked Bert politely.

"Not so fast, boy, not so fast," the prospector's rasping voice warned him. "I'm not sure that I want you to go down and talk about my mine. Maybe you'd better stay up here with me tonight while we talk things over."

"Oh, I don't think I should," Bert said. A twinge of fear shot through him, but was quickly succeeded by a feeling of resolution. He looked frantically at the stool on which the candle was burning feebly. With one backward kick of his foot he knocked it over again. As darkness succeeded light, and a roar of anger came from the tunnel behind him, he dived out the door and into the flying whiteness of late afternoon.

Ignoring the path, he plunged downhill, waist deep in snow. Gasping and floundering, he soon outdistanced the prospector, but fear impelled him to struggle on as long as he could. Ahead of him was nothing but a white blur. He wallowed forward through a screen of spruce, and then the snow gave way under him. He shot out into space. In his mind was the agonizing thought that he was doomed. Then he dropped into a feathery mass. It absorbed his body and drew him down as if he had dived into a deep pool of water. Struggling and sputtering, he pulled himself back into the light again, staggered to his feet, and looked uphill. Behind him was a forty-foot cliff.

"Wow!" he said to himself. "That was a close one!" He felt in his shirt. The lump of rock was still cold against his skin. Ahead, the curtain of falling snow blocked off his view. Suddenly he heard a familiar sound, a click-click-click. It took him a minute to figure out what it was, and then he gave a yell. The click was the sound of automobile chains. The road must be just below!

A Visit With the Sheriff

Inside the shower stall the water poured down in a refreshing torrent and baked the soreness from Bert's leg muscles. He was content to relax and to let the steaming flood wash away the tiredness that had permeated his brain and body.

Suddenly the shower curtain was pulled aside, and Howard stuck in his blond head. "Hey," he said, "what happened? Ed and I got back a little while ago, and the clerk told us you'd come through the lobby looking as if a ghost were after you, or as if you'd been caught in an avalanche."

Bert reached up swiftly and twisted the shower head so that its full force came down on Howard's upturned face.

As his brother withdrew, he chuckled and then shouted above the roar of the water, "It wasn't an avalanche that caught me, dope! It was a flood!"

Howard sputtered indignantly, furiously toweling his dripping head. "See you later," he yelled at his brother. "I have an errand to perform."

"I'm lucky," Bert thought to himself. "I'm a lucky guy. I might still be up in that cave if I hadn't had sense enough to bolt and run for it."

A moment later the water, at first refreshing, suddenly turned to live steam. It was unbearably hot and Bert fiddled frantically with the control levers of the shower. He turned the cold lever on full, but still nothing happened, and he fled hastily to the cool air of the bunkroom, shivering and dripping. Behind him the shower sent out a cloud of steam.

"Doggone it all!" he grumbled, as he grabbed for a towel to wipe his eyes. Water, dripping from his body, was forming a puddle on the rug. As he rubbed the towel over his damp hair, he looked toward the door. Howard stood there, a suspicious smirk on his face.

"I guess that evens things up," he said calmly to Bert. "I just turned off the cold water valve down in the basement for a moment. It's back on now."

Bert let out a whoop and started across the room, the towel in his hands. He managed to snap it just once at the retreating figure of his brother before Howard, his eyes twinkling and his snub nose tilted triumphantly upward, made an exit through the swinging doors to the hall.

Bert broke into a laugh. It was the signal that brought Howard back from the hall to ask eagerly, "Well, what *did* happen? You still haven't told me. We were just about ready to send out the posse when you showed up."

"Take it easy," protested Bert, who had one leg in his trousers and one leg outside. "Bring Ed up here, and I'll tell you both all about it."

He hastily selected a clean shirt from the dresser drawer, and was giving his damp hair a lick and a promise before the mirror when he saw Ed's lanky figure and serious face reflected from the doorway.

"Hi," he said casually and continued brushing back the troublesome, red cowlick that he never seemed to be able to keep pasted into place on the back of his head.

"Hi, yourself," replied his older brother in a tone that was, Bert reflected, somewhat disapproving. He swung around and saw on Ed's face the look that his older brother always reserved for him when he had gotten himself in some particularly disconcerting scrape. Dropping the comb and brush, Bert draped himself across the nearest bunk.

"Well, boys, it's a long story," he began. "But you remember the old prospector who was hanging around the blackboard at the foot of the lift yesterday? The one who might have rubbed out the avalanche warnings? Well—"

Swiftly he sketched in the outline of the story.

"Boy, you're going to take one chance too many some of these days," Ed finally observed, and Bert's gay pride shriveled under the weight of his disapproving words. "Someday you're going to run off without telling anyone, and then it'll be curtains for you. All I have to say is—cut it out! And don't go gallivanting around like that again, ever. At least, if you get some crazy idea, cut us in on it."

"But it wasn't completely crazy, Ed," protested Bert. To prove his point he reached under the bed and brought out the piece of rock he had carried away from Skeleton Cave. "Look what I found."

"What is it?" Ed asked scornfully. He had been stampeded before by Bert's enthusiasm, and now he was a little skeptical.

Bert held the hunk of gold in his fingers, turning the glittering side so that it reflected the light from the lamp. "Gold," said Bert calmly, "from Skeleton Cave."

"Yipe!" shouted Howard, springing up from his chair

and rushing over to grab the chunk of stone. "Then you found Uncle John's lost mine!"

"Well, it does look that way," said Bert, calm in his triumph. "See those little yellow particles? I'd say they're gold, wouldn't you?"

As he spoke, he saw Ed rising from his chair and strolling across the room.

"It does look as if you found something," his older brother admitted, tossing the hunk of rock from one hand to another. "Maybe I ought to apologize. But now what I want to know is, how are we ever going to be able to find that mine again?"

Bert ruefully contemplated the piece of rock as his brother handed it back to him. He shook his head before replying. "That's going to be a problem," he said, "but perhaps Mr. Wilson will have some suggestions when he comes up again."

"Why, he's downstairs right now," Howard broke in. "At least, he phoned this afternoon and said he'd be up to join us for dinner."

"In that case," said Bert, "I'll just wrap this hunk of gold in a handkerchief and take it down to show to him. Boy, I'll bet he'll be surprised!"

Clutching the precious rock in his right hand, he led the way out the door and sprinted down the steps into the living room. Mr. Wilson, still in his familiar tweeds, looked up at him from one sofa, Alan Wallace from another. Repressing his temptation to blurt out the secret, Bert nodded at Alan, smiled at Mr. Wilson, and strolled in to the dinner table with the lawyer.

This night, for a change, he did not feel like lingering over his meal. He gulped his soup, wolfed down his meat, hurried through his dessert, and then discovered that he was one course ahead of Mr. Wilson and his brothers. Squirming impatiently, he waited for the meal to end and the other guests to leave the dining room. At last they were alone. The plates had been cleared away, and the waitresses had retired through the swinging doors into the kitchen.

Lifting one corner of his blue bandanna handkerchief, Bert nudged Mr. Wilson, who looked down at what the boy was holding in his hands. As Bert watched, the lawyer's eyebrows rose. He picked up the chunk of rock and inspected it closely.

"I've found Uncle John's mine!" Bert finally burst out after an appropriate period of silence had passed. "It's up

on Panorama Gap, just as you said!"

Mr. Wilson seemed to be paying very little attention to what Bert said. He pulled a pocket knife from his trousers and scraped very delicately at one fleck of glittering substance on the surface of the rock.

"Was there a lot of this rock where you found this chunk?" he finally inquired.

"Tons of it!" Bert said. "I went up with old Willis King, the crazy prospector, and he showed me great big piles of gold, lying all over the inside of a cave."

"Did you say gold?" asked Mr. Wilson, turning to face Bert.

"Yes, real gold!" said Bert. "See, you've just been scraping flecks of it loose."

A strange look came across the lawyer's face. "This isn't gold, Bert," the lawyer said pityingly. "It's fool's gold, and it's not worth a cent a ton. Not a cent a ton."

Bert gulped to swallow the lump in his throat. He couldn't bear to look at his brothers. He dropped his eyes and stared down at the table.

"But—but Willis King said it was real," he protested.

"Yes," the lawyer said compassionately, "and now you must know that Willis King is not in his right mind. That's why everybody feels sorry for him. He keeps saying that he's rich. Actually, he isn't worth a penny."

"Then Uncle John's mine is worthless?" asked Bert sadly.

"Not necessarily," said Mr. Wilson, an encouraging note in his deep voice. "As I understand it, your Uncle John did a lot of prospecting in this area. The Skeleton Mine is in one of the areas he visited, of that I'm sure, but it may not be the only mine he opened up. In fact, we still have to explore over on Mount Holliss. And what's more, we have to see if we can find the records from the old town hall."

Bert brightened a little at the prospect of snatching victory from defeat.

"What do we do next?" he asked eagerly, daring to look at Mr. Wilson again.

"I think we'd better go down and see the sheriff of Sunmount," he said. "He may be able to help us."

"Who's the sheriff?" asked Bert. "And why does Sunmount need a sheriff anyway?"

"It's just a courtesy title," Mr. Wilson replied. "He's an old gentleman now, but years ago he actually was the sheriff here. In fact, he's one of the few people that survived the big avalanche that wiped out the town."

"Where does he live?" Bert inquired. He was beginning to be interested in this new character.

"Just above the road," the lawyer said. "Maybe you've noticed smoke coming out a chimney that just sticks out above the snow."

"I have," said Howard, "and I wondered what it was."

"Well, that's the sheriff's home," said the lawyer. "The snow is so deep up here in the wintertime that you have to climb down a ladder through a hole in the roof."

"Sounds like fun," Bert said. "Can we go over there tonight?"

"Why, sure," said the lawyer. "Get your boots on, and we'll go across now. I'm sure he's home."

Bert strolled away from the table and sprinted upstairs, his brothers following him. He was wearing slippers, because his feet hurt; but he slipped back into his ski boots, tying the laces loosely. Mr. Wilson was standing by the door when he came down, and Alan was still sitting by himself in a chair near the fireplace. On his face there was a smug expression.

"Like a cat that's swallowed a canary," Bert thought bitterly as he scuffed across the floor and followed the others into the snowy night.

10   *The Search for the Records*

The beam of the flashlight picked out the smoke rising from the sheriff's chimney. The storm was ending, and the moon shone fitfully between scuds of cloud whisking across the sky. Bert was glad the path was firm underfoot.

"Okay, boys," the voice of Mr. Wilson floated back to him. "Here we are. And watch your step, please." The lawyer pounded on a trap door that rose above the snow alongside the chimney. From somewhere down in the earth came back a muffled roar. Mr. Wilson flung open the door.

"Brought you some visitors, Sheriff," he shouted down into the cavern. "This is Charley Wilson. Can we come in?"

"Sure," came the jovial rumble from below. "Bring 'em down. But mind the ladder."

Bert waited until the lawyer was out of sight and then lowered himself gingerly through the trap door. His feet slipped on the smooth rungs of a ladder that descended toward a pool of light. As he climbed down, he could see Ed's legs above him. At the bottom of the ladder he found himself in a tiny anteroom. Its walls were plastered with old newspapers. He waited a moment until his brothers had joined him and then walked through an open door into a comfortable living room.

As Bert entered, a stout, gray-haired man with a ruddy face rose and stuck out his hand. Bert grasped it and winced at the strength of the handshake.

"I'm the sheriff," the red-faced man rumbled. "Make yourself comfortable, boys." He waved toward three nail kegs, which apparently served as living-room chairs. The only soft piece of furniture in the house was the sofa, on which he sat with Mr. Wilson.

"Now, what's botherin' you, Charley?" he demanded of Mr. Wilson.

From his uneasy perch, Bert saw the lawyer lean forward to answer with another question, "Can you keep a secret, Sheriff? A big one?"

"Why, of course," the sheriff said indignantly. "Nobody ever accused me of blabbin' somethin' I was s'posed to keep to myself."

"Well, then, I'll let Bert, here, tell you his story," the lawyer said. He nodded at Bert.

Across the room a single log was blazing in the fireplace. As Bert went along with his story, he saw the sheriff prick up his ears with interest. It took him many minutes to complete the recitation. As he finished, the log on the hearth split in two and dropped with a faint crash from the andirons that had been holding it.

"Well, now," said the sheriff benevolently, "maybe I *can* help you. So happens I remember a man who might have been your Uncle John—a quiet feller, came from New England in the late nineties. He did a lot of moseyin' around here, but far's I know it never came to anythin'. We all did a lot of lookin' for gold, and we found everythin' else but —silver, bismuth, and a lot of other metals, but so far no gold."

"You mean there's no gold in this valley?" Bert asked, striving to keep the disappointment out of his voice.

"Wait a minute, son! Wait a minute!" said the sheriff, holding up one hand. "I didn't say there wasn't gold in this valley; I just said that we never found any. I do know that there's gold in the valley just to the north of us. There's a couple of big mines over on that side, and I've figured there ought to be gold over here too. Just never happened to find it."

"Well, do you think the Wallaces have found gold?" Bert inquired slowly.

"I don't just know what to think about those fellers," the sheriff answered. "Old Tom and his boy, Alan. They act around here as if they're poor, but a friend of mine down in the city—he's seen old Tom visitin' the assay office a couple of times with a big bag under his arm—might have gold dust in it. Ever' so often he takes the train out of Salt Lake and goes somewhere.

"Trips cost money, and sendin' his boy East to school must have cost him a pile of money. And yet he drives around here in an old jalopy as if he didn't have two nickels to rub together. I say, I can't figure it out."

Bert squirmed restlessly on his barrel perch and ran one hand through his flaming hair. He could hardly wait for the sheriff to stop talking.

"The thing we need most of all, Sheriff," he said, "is the mining record from the old courthouse at Sunmount— the record of claims filed. That'll tell us if Uncle John did file a claim on a gold mine; and, if so, where it is. But we understand that those records were lost in the avalanche."

"That's right," agreed the sheriff, hooking one thumb under the galluses that held up his trousers. "The records *was* lost. Nobody cared much, 'cause most all the claims had also been registered down in the city. But—come to think of it—" He paused and scratched his head.

"Come to think of what?" Bert prompted him. The sheriff delayed his answer for a moment. Then he brought one hamlike hand down on his knee with a sharp, slapping sound.

"By gracious, I'll bet that's the answer!" he said. "Right after the avalanche, when we were diggin' ourselves out, I met up with old Tom Wallace prowlin' around the courthouse. It was only a wood building, and it'd been knocked flat. I asked him what he was doin' there, and he said somethin' about gettin' a few boards to build himself a new house. He'd been up in the hills and had missed the slide."

"I don't think I understand what you're driving at, Sheriff," Ed's calm voice broke in. "What is it you're trying to tell us?"

"Simple, boy, simple," said the sheriff with an expansive gesture. "Mebbe Tom Wallace wasn't lookin' for boards. Mebbe he was lookin' for the minin' records. And—" he paused to let his words sink in—"mebbe he found 'em."

On the snowy road outside, Bert shook hands with Mr. Wilson, and then guided the beam of the flashlight so the lawyer could back his car out of the parking area and turn it around. The lights of the car clicked on, illuminating the glittering snow, and, with a wave of the hand, Mr. Wilson shifted into low gear and started away.

"Well, that's something to dream on," said Ed, stifling a yawn. "Now suppose we go to bed." With Bert and Howard trailing him he clattered down the covered passageway to the Chalet terrace. He was about to push open the door when Bert reached forward and touched his arm.

"See what I see?" whispered Bert. Inside by the dying fire Alan was asleep in his chair. A book, its pages fluttering in a faint breeze, lay on his lap.

"Yeah," said Ed. "Let's tiptoe in. No sense waking him. He can sleep there about as well as he can down at his own house."

"No," Bert whispered back, "I've got a better idea. Just follow me a minute."

The three boys tiptoed around the edge of the terrace and out of hearing of the living room.

"Now, listen," said Bert sharply. "Maybe this is taking too much of a chance, but we've got to stick our necks out somewhere along the line. We've got to know whether those mining records are in the Wallace house. I think we ought to ski down there now and take a quick look around. Mr. Wallace is away, and this is our chance."

"Don't be silly," Ed answered him. "Suppose we get caught?"

"We can handle that," Bert reassured him. "We'll post you as sentry. Remember the owl hoot we used to give at camp back in Maine when we were playing cops and robbers? Well, you just hoot if you spy anyone. Howard and I'll go down into the house and see what we can see. We'll leave the trap door open so we can hear you."

A moment later they were skimming down the hill toward the Wallace cabin.

Shadowed by trees the cabin gave off no sign of life. No smoke curled from the chimney. The snow, pale white in the shifting moonlight, was marked by a single pair of ski tracks—obviously Alan's, Bert decided. At the edge of the grove he stopped.

"You stay here, just inside the tree line," he whispered hoarsely. "If Mr. Wallace comes back, he most likely will come by the Chalet first, and on foot, so keep watching that way. Howard and I will go on."

The Wallace cabin lay just ahead. Here in the trees the snow had not drifted quite so deeply. Banks of white rose to the middle of the second-floor windows, and there was a gleam of glass reflecting the snow piled alongside them.

"He must have a trap door like the sheriff's," Bert reflected to himself. He looked up at the steeply sloping roof. On one side thin boards had been placed vertically as cleats—obviously leading to the trap door.

"You stay by my skis," he said quietly to Howard, who nodded obediently. He reached down and loosened the front clamps, then kicked off his skis and stood them in the snow. With one last look around he started up the ladder of cleats.

"Hey, what goes on?" a hoarse and angry voice shouted from the edge of the grove—the edge toward the lift. From the other side of the grove came a soft, hooting sound. Bert froze into stillness.

"Who's there?" the angry voice demanded.

Bert swung over on his back and slid down over the bumpy cleats. He kicked his boots into his ski bindings without bothering to tighten the heel springs and shouted, "Let's go!"

He dived forward as the ground dropped away steeply

in front of him, and swung down a little hill through the trees, more by instinct than by knowledge of the terrain. He was going away from the lift and away from Ed as well. But Ed would know how to get away, he thought to himself.

A flame split the darkness, and there was a roar overhead.

"Good grief, he's shooting at us!" he flung over his shoulder at Howard. His younger brother was swinging down behind him. Suddenly the slope dropped away. "I don't know what's below," he said frantically to himself, "but here goes nothing." A moment later he was waist deep in water. There was a splash as Howard lit beside him.

"Take your skis off and wade!" he said sharply. He could hear Howard's teeth rattling as his younger brother bent down and put his mittened hands under water to loosen the ski bindings. Somewhere up the hill he could hear a man puffing and breathing heavily—Alan's father, no doubt, wallowing down through the snow.

The water struck a chill into Bert's bones, but he doggedly waded up against the current. He knew now where he was. A swift-flowing brook poured down off the mountain on one side of the chair lift and then flowed down the valley. They were following that brook.

11   *Up the Mountainside*

The sound of a sneeze woke Bert, and he shook his head drowsily, trying to figure where the noise came from.

"Ahh-choo!" It was Howard, all right. Bert groped drowsily for his left pajama sleeve and slipped it back to peer at the time. The luminous dial blinked back at him. It was six thirty. He dropped back on the pillow and lay there a moment.

Bert yawned luxuriously. In the middle of his yawn a bell began to ring, far off but insistently. He swung his bare feet out of bed and lit with a thump on the chilly floor.

"Breakfast!" he yelled.

Ed awoke slowly. Howard reached for a handkerchief under his pillow, and blew his nose with a stentorian sound.

"I feel punk," the younger boy announced, and went back to sleep again.

"No wonder," observed Ed sharply.

Bert dropped his eyes as his brother looked accusingly at him, and then said, "Well, gee whiz! It was a chance worth taking, wasn't it?" He looked up just in time to see his older brother shaking his head reproachfully.

"Never again," Ed said clearly. "That's the last escapade you'll ever take me on. Beginning today let's be a little more sensible."

"Okay, okay," Bert said hastily and eagerly. "I was wrong and I admit it."

"Then let's go to breakfast and have a tray sent up for Howard," said his older brother, swinging open the door that led to the hallway. He led the way with long strides through the living room, but hesitated momentarily at the entrance to the dining room. Bert, just behind Ed, heard him exclaim, "Hi, there!"

As Bert walked into the dining room, he saw the reason for the greeting. Muldrow Holliday, tanned and smiling, sat at one of the small tables. The two boys quickly sat down beside him.

"I heard some shootin' last night," the ranger drawled, "and I thought I'd ask you what it was all about."

Bert looked around the room to make sure that Alan

wasn't there, then launched spiritedly into his explanation. He was interrupted several times as a waitress stopped
at his elbow to inquire what he wanted to eat and to take his
own order and that of his sick brother. Finally, however,
talking in an urgent undertone, he finished his story of
the night's events and leaned back to see how Mr. Holliday
was reacting. To his relief the ranger only smiled.

"It was a long chance," he said, "and I certainly don't
believe in prying into other people's affairs. So I can't say
that I approve, but I'm certainly glad you got out of the
whole mess without being shot."

"That's the way I feel," agreed Bert, passing a hand over
his hair. "But the next question is, where do we go from
here?"

"I've got an answer to that," answered the ranger. He
pointed down to his feet, and alongside them Bert's eager
eyes caught sight of a coil of rope.

"What's that for?" he asked.

"I thought we might go climbing today," answered the
ranger. "Wait till we get outside and I'll tell you about it.
That is, if you're game."

"Well, of course!" said Bert. The two boys rose from the
table, following Holliday, and scuffed across the living

room, where half a dozen guests were relaxing. The terrace door squeaked as they swung it open and stepped out into the morning's cold.

"It's a good day for rock climbing," elaborated Holliday as he carelessly swung the rope from one hand to the other. "I brought a rope, and if you fellows have some rubber-soled shoes, we might go up the rocks to Stampede Tunnel and explore a bit."

"Where's that?" asked Bert, shading his eyes against the fierce glare of the sun as he looked off in the direction Holliday had indicated.

"Up in the neighborhood of your Skeleton Mine," said Holliday. "There's a network of old mining tunnels up there. Stampede Tunnel is the biggest. It goes right through the mountain to the other side. It occurred to me that your Skeleton Mine, or Cave, might somehow be linked up with it by a side tunnel. Anyway you'll get to see the other side of the mountain."

"But we don't know anything about climbing," protested Bert.

"That doesn't matter too much," said the ranger. "Really, it's more of a scramble than a rock climb, except in a couple of places. I'll lead on the rope, and I can hold both of you at once—assuming you slipped or fell, which I'm sure you won't."

"Okay with me," said Bert, shoving both hands into his pockets but secretly quaking a little at the thought of climbing the cliffs he could see so clearly. He looked hopefully at Ed.

"Okay," Ed finally said. "We'll go. As long as you're with us, we won't get into trouble."

It seemed less than five minutes later, but it must have been much longer, when Bert and Ed reappeared on the front terrace. On their feet were stout rubber-soled hiking shoes. Each boy wore a warm jacket. They hadn't bothered with lunches, and they didn't need to. On Holliday's back was a rucksack in which were sandwiches and a Thermos of cocoa.

"We'll walk up to my cabin, just as if we were going to talk over some business," he said to Bert, "and we'll start up the rocks behind it."

"But why go up the rocks?" asked Bert. "Wouldn't it be easier to take our skis and go up the snow?"

"It would," said Holliday, "but already there have been two small avalanches up there. See those two gullies where the snow's slid away? That's bad country for avalanches. At least on the rocks we're sure to be safe."

Bert looked up the path, past the ranger's log cabin, to the yellow and broken cliffs beyond. His eye followed the line of the cliffs upward to a dark opening in the middle of a snow patch and what might have been an old road winding down from it.

"There?" he asked, touching the ranger's arm.

Holliday nodded. "That's the mine," he said. "How far above us would you guess it is?"

"A mile?" hazarded Bert, hopefully.

Holliday shook his head. "Your eyesight plays tricks in this wide-open country," he said. "It's a good three miles and about three thousand vertical feet above us. And here's where we begin to climb.

"I'll tie in you two boys," the ranger said. He rose, walked over to Bert, and looped the rope around him. His flying fingers tied a stout knot, which he tightened so that Bert could feel the pressure of the strands on his chest. Then carefully uncoiling the rope, Holliday located its middle and tied another loop, which he dropped over Ed's head and then tightened around the latter's chest.

"Just keep track of where I go," said Holliday, "and you'll be all right. On this easy stuff all of us can climb at once. When the going gets tougher, I'll tell you and we'll climb one at a time."

"But what do we do if the rope gets snarled?" inquired Bert, who was beginning to lose his taste for rock climbing even before he started.

"Oh, that's all right," said the ranger. "Just take a few coils of rope in your hand and see that not too much slack exists between any of us." He started nimbly up the rock.

"Okay," said Bert, swallowing hard. "Here goes." He began to scramble up over the rock.

The party gained altitude rapidly. Now and then they had to wallow through deep drifts where snow had collected. By craning his neck, Bert discovered that he could see the Chalet, now rapidly lessening in size. Along the track to Tom Wallace's house he could see a dark figure moving slowly. The broad highway looked like a ribbon.

Ahead of him, Holliday had halted. Bert panted upward, occasionally dislodging a rock. Finally he dropped with a sigh on a projecting boulder a few feet away from the ranger. He was breathing hard, his face was flushed, and tiny drops of perspiration stood out on his ruddy forehead.

"I guess I don't know the secret of this kind of climbing," he confessed.

The ranger grinned at him. "Just take it easy," said Holliday. "Don't rush. Make sure of your footing. That's all you need to do." The ranger rose, craned his neck, and looked up at the cliff that barred his way. "Nothing difficult here," he observed, "but we'd better climb one at a time. You boys watch closely, and go where I do. I'll pick a good stance up above and support you on the rope as each of you comes up." He began to move deliberately up the cliff. To Bert it seemed as if the rocks actually hung out over his head, but he noticed that Holliday was moving steadily upward. Finally the ranger swung himself over the top of a ledge and disappeared from sight. A moment later a yodel floated down and then a faint "All right!"

"That's you," Bert said to his brother. "Holler down when you want me to start." He noticed that Ed looked a little pale, but he also noticed that his older brother was moving steadily upward. Once or twice Bert could see from his perch below that Ed was groping for holds. The rope from above was taut, and as Ed climbed, it kept pace with him. Then Bert could see his brother's legs against the blue sky, and finally nothing at all, as Ed disappeared from sight.

Down there, at the bottom of the cliff, he seemed to be more alone than ever before in his life. The rocks plunged out beneath his feet, and plummeted down into the valley, where the buildings seemed to be the size of doll houses. The cliff, as Bert looked at it, seemed to be tipping toward him. For once in his life, he was frightened.

"Okay!" came his brother's baritone voice, and the echo bounced from the cliffs. The rope tightened around Bert's chest, and he began to climb. There was nothing really substantial on which to rest his feet, and once or twice he struggled to keep his footing. But the cliff was less steep than he had thought. Now and then there were ledges where he could straighten his legs, and always there was the rope, supporting him from above.

Just above him was a wide opening in the rock. He wriggled into this broad crack. Loose fragments lay on its lower side, and Bert dislodged a few pieces as he struggled up toward the blue sky and sunlight he could see just ahead.

"Just a few feet more!" he heard a voice say above him, and then he was out in the sunlight, scrambling onto a broad ledge and gasping like a fish from the effort he had put into his climb. Holliday winked at him and said, "Take it easy, boy. We've still got a ways to go."

"Good grief!" panted Bert. "With more cliffs like that last one?"

"Well, maybe one more," said the ranger reassuringly. "But mostly it's just scrambling."

"Boy, I'll never be afraid of high buildings again!" said Bert, and there was a heartfelt note in his voice. "Nothing could be much tougher than this."

"Well, let's get going," said the ranger. "We've still got some distance to cover."

The rest of the trip was a blur to Bert. There were masses of jagged, broken rock piled every which way, only waiting for a careless footstep to send them thundering down into the valley; another sheer cliff; and finally a tremendous slope of loose gravel in which, it seemed to Bert, he slid backward two steps for every one he took forward.

"Here we are!" The voice of Muldrow Holliday floated down to him. Bert rubbed his eyes with a grimy hand and looked up the slope. Fifty feet ahead it leveled out. At the far end of this space a black spot showed in the face of the dun-colored rock. They had reached the tunnel.

12   *In the Tunnel*

From his pack, Muldrow Holliday withdrew a flashlight. He clicked it on and glanced at the weak flicker of the bulb, pale beside the sunlight that flooded the entranceway. Bert, watching him, felt more confidence than ever in Holliday's leadership.

"How about some lunch?" the ranger inquired. He drew two paper bags from his pack and handed one each to Bert and Ed. Then, after withdrawing a third bag, he pulled out a Thermos bottle and two tin cups, into which he poured steaming cocoa.

"I'm going to hate to get out of this sunlight," Bert remarked to Holliday. "I'll bet it'll be cold inside the tunnel."

"No, not too cold," the ranger said. "The temperature seems to stay at an even fifty degrees in there—cool, but not really chilly. It's a little wet, though, and a good mile through to the other side."

"Then as soon as we've eaten, we'd better get going, hadn't we?" asked Bert. "We don't want to get benighted on the mountainside." His glance fell on a narrow little path, free in part from snow, that wound across the slope and disappeared into a clump of trees.

"That's an old miner's path," said Holliday, who was watching him. "It's slid away a little farther on, and it goes under some avalanche slopes. In the summertime it would be a good way to get up here."

"That means we've got to go down the same way we came up, doesn't it?" Bert asked glumly. He had no relish for a descent over the rocks.

"Why, sure!" Holliday said heartily, and his face crinkled into a smile. "Don't take it so hard, Bert. A few more climbs like this one, and you'll be an experienced rock climber."

The beam of Holliday's flashlight illuminated walls dripping with moisture and picked out a rusty railroad track. The patch of sunlight dwindled to pin-point size and then faded altogether, as Bert and his brother followed the ranger along through the tunnel. It was, as Holliday had said, not too cold in the dark interior.

At one point the tunnel curved sharply to the right, and another tunnel forked to the left. Holliday stopped a minute, and then said, "We'd better explore both these tunnels. No telling where they'll lead."

"But hadn't you better leave the rope behind as sort of a marker?" asked Bert.

Holliday chuckled. "I left that out at the entrance," he said. "Too heavy to carry."

The right-hand tunnel, which they turned into, began to narrow and finally ended in a mass of tumbled, jagged boulders. Carefully they retraced their steps.

"Looks as if we'll have to go the other way," said Holliday. "It's going to take a little squirming before we get out. There's been a rockfall, but we can squeeze under it."

As he spoke, the flashlight beam illuminated the corner the boys had just left. They swung off in the other direction. The sound of their footsteps echoed weirdly in Bert's ears, and he panted as he tried to match his legs against Holliday's long stride.

It seemed to Bert as if he had been walking for miles. Occasionally he looked around to reassure himself that Ed still was following him. He could see Holliday's checked

shirt in the dim light, but he stumbled forward against the ranger when Holliday suddenly came to a halt. The flashlight played on a pile of boulders, which seemed to fill the tunnel from wall to wall.

"Don't worry," came back Holliday's reassuring voice. "Look here." His beam lit up a hole in the rock alongside one wall, just big enough for a man to wriggle through. He handed the flashlight back to Bert, got down on his hands and knees, and disappeared into the darkness.

"Come on through!" his voice floated back. Bert flashed the light on the hole in the boulder pile and then dropped down to crawl through. It was a close fit, and when he touched a boulder at one side, it seemed to quiver as if it were about to move. He had left the flashlight behind, and now he could see its beam shining faintly as Ed followed him through the hole.

"It's not far now," Holliday said. "See there?" Ahead of them there was a dot of light. "That's the other end of the tunnel," the ranger said. "We'll be there in five minutes. Can't go down to the valley that way because of avalanches, but at least we can look over the edge."

Bert thought that he had never in his life been so grateful for sunlight and fresh air.

"Well, that's that," said Holliday. "No hidden gold mines. At least we've cleared up this particular mystery."

"And now we're almost back where we started," Bert remarked wryly. "Except for Mount Holliss. And that's across the other valley."

"Well, at least we had a nice trip," remarked Holliday.

Bert looked at his watch and stifled an exclamation. It was three o'clock, and by six it would be dark! Holliday cocked his head and took a look at the watch dial. "Better be getting back," he remarked.

As Bert started back into the tunnel, he could hear a rumbling noise ahead. The sound grew louder, rushed out toward him, echoed from mountainside to mountainside. He stole a look at the ranger. Holliday's face was ashy.

"That sounds like our rock pile going!" Bert said hoarsely. He felt a prickling at the roots of his hair.

The three of them stumbled back through the tunnel. The flashlight beam, bright when they started the trip, was rapidly dimming, and Holliday shook the light once or twice with alarm.

"Guess we must have loosened some of the rocks crawling through," he said. "But I can still see a little cranny there. Maybe, if we're lucky, we can pry away enough rocks to wiggle through. You kids stand back and hold the flash-light. I'm going to try it."

"Do you need light now?" Bert asked, as he felt the cold metal of the flashlight against his outstretched palm.

"Well, only now and then," the ranger said. "We'd better conserve the battery."

By now Holliday was on his stomach, prying away rocks.

"Be ready to drag me back if the rocks start to roll," he flung back over his shoulder. Ed dropped to his knees in back of the ranger and kept his hands on Holliday's putteed legs. In the darkness there was a grating sound as Holliday worked frantically at the boulders.

Then there was silence. Bert could hear the ranger's deep, husky breathing and the subdued clatter of rocks. Finally the ranger said in a casual tone of voice, "Okay, now, if you're careful. I've got a route through, but you'll have to be sure not to disturb the boulders on either side. Some of them are pretty loose."

"Well, here goes," said Bert, handing the flashlight back to Ed. "Guess it's our last chance." The damp floor of the tunnel struck a chill into his chest as he wriggled into the passageway, delicately touching the rocks on either side with his outstretched fingers. It seemed hours, but actually only minutes passed until he felt strong hands on his shoulders and was literally yanked through the last few feet of the hole. Panting a little from the tension of the crawl, Bert moved off to one side.

"Let him make it," he prayed silently. "Please, oh please, let him through."

He could hear Ed's slow movements through the boulder pile. He clicked on the light as Holliday bent forward and grabbed Ed's shoulders. Then, as he watched, one of Ed's boots caught on a projecting rock. It began to move.

"Look out!" Bert shouted, but before he had the words out of his mouth, the ranger had yanked Ed to freedom much as he might have pulled in a fish. And behind them, with a roar, a new cascade of rocks streamed down.

"That finishes it," said Holliday, wiping the perspiration from his forehead. "Nobody will be going through that tunnel again for a long, long time."

Bert exhaled with a long, sighing sound. "Okay," he said, "let's get going," and they took up their stumbling march toward the other end of the tunnel.

As they rounded a corner, they could see the sunlight far off in the distance. It grew larger as they moved along, and, just as the mountains beyond began to show up clearly, the flashlight gave out.

"Lucky," said Bert. "We made it. That's all that counts."

"Sure is," said the ranger. "Now we'll have to make time going down the mountain." He stepped out in front and took a few paces into the sunlight.

"Hey—" he began.

Bert walked out into the sunlight and asked, "What's happened?"

"Our rope," said the ranger softly. "It's gone!"

Across the valley the red ball of the sun had dropped behind the spiky mountain peaks, rimming them with fire. Already the chill of the high places was in the air.

Something like despair came into Bert's voice "What are we going to do?" he asked. "What *can* we do?" His voice trembled, and he looked at the rock walls below.

"There's only one answer," said the ranger grimly, "and it may not be pleasant for you."

"Well, tell us anyway," urged Ed, standing shoulder to shoulder with Bert.

"I'll have to go down by myself," said the ranger. "I can make it, but I can't take you boys down without a rope. You'll have to spend the night up here in the tunnel. It may be uncomfortable, but you'll survive. You can build a fire. In the morning I'll be back up to get you."

"Well, okay," Bert said stoutly. "Only I wonder what became of the rope?"

"Obvious," said the ranger bitterly. He swung one hand toward the path leading across the snow slopes. "See those footprints? Somebody came up, took a chance on the avalanche slopes, and swiped the rope."

"I'll bet I know who it was," said Bert. "I'll bet it was one of the Wallaces."

"Or maybe the old prospector, or maybe somebody we've never even met," Ed contributed. "That's beside the point right now. What we've got to do is figure why he did it."

"My guess is that he hoped you wouldn't be able to climb down again," said the ranger. "He probably figured you boys came up here alone. He knows you've taken some chances already, whoever your enemy is, and if you'd been alone, I doubt that you would have gotten down. Between the cliffs and the avalanches it would have been less than a fifty-fifty chance."

"Well, we'd better settle down," said Bert. "There's some timber here, and I've got a hunting knife, so we can make a pretty good fire."

"And I've still got three sandwiches," said the ranger, "which I'll leave with you."

Against the dimming light of dusk, Holliday's craggy face looked as if it had been chiseled from rock. His head was turned toward the cliffs below, and his eyes were fixed on the route they had climbed.

"Well, so long," he said finally. "I'd better get moving." He clattered down the gravel slope, and the boys watched until he was out of sight.

"There's a brave man," said Bert finally. He swung around and picked up a heavy timber, bleached gray from wind, snow and rain.

"Let's get going," he flung at his brother. "At least we'll keep warm tonight."

13   *A Trip to Castle Rock*

Sometime before dawn Bert woke from his fitful sleep. His neck was stiff and his right hand and arm, on which he had slept, were cramped and tingling.

He painfully uncoiled himself and looked around at Ed, still asleep. With difficulty Bert turned his head; his eyes were still thickened by sleep. Outside everything was gray and a little misty.

Bert stretched himself out on the scattered boughs, tucked his arm under him; and, before he knew it, was asleep again. His last thought was that he must have been very tired to doze off so quickly.

In his dream, which was a long and wild one, Bert seemed to hear someone shouting. He tried feebly to answer, but he didn't seem to be able to make his voice carry to whoever was calling him. Then somebody was shaking him, and he looked up to see Holliday smiling down at him.

"I'm a little late," said the ranger, "but still in plenty of time. It's going to snow, but not until after we get down off the mountain."

Bert stretched himself and yawned luxuriously. Ed already was sitting up.

"I feel as if I were ninety years old," Bert said sleepily, struggling to his feet. He rubbed his eyes with his knuckles.

Holliday lifted a climbing rope from his rucksack, hefted it tenderly, and then began the delicate job of uncoiling. He dropped the strands to the floor of the cave in wavy loops and tied the two boys in.

"This time, for safety, you boys go ahead of me," he said. "Then if you slip, I can hold you from behind. You first, Bert!"

The gravel slid away with a hissing sound as the three climbers began to drop down toward the valley. Once Bert lost his footing and sat down. He could hear the others chuckling as they saw the surprised expression on his face.

"Don't let this scree worry you," the ranger said to him. "Just slide with it. There's a broad ledge down below, and if you want to have some fun, we can just run down. Keep your heels well dug in and knees bent, and slide with the scree." He plunged out ahead, and the two boys, whooping and yelling, followed him. They all slid to a halt on a grassy plateau, just at the top of the first big cliff.

"This won't be too bad," said Holliday, anticipating Bert's thoughts, "Just face in toward the cliff. Keep your body out, look over your shoulder for the next foothold, and don't let your feet get too far below your hands. In other words, when you move your feet down, move your hands too. That way you'll never be out of balance."

It seemed to Bert that he couldn't possibly muster up the will power to turn around, facing Holliday, and to reach out over the edge of the cliff with his feet, searching for holds. But finally he summoned up his courage and began the climb down. The nervousness he felt must have showed in his wide eyes for Holliday gave him a reassuring wink. Encouraged, Bert began to drop swiftly down toward another ledge not too far below. He knew that he must test each place where he put his hands and feet, to make sure that the rock was solid.

Once, however, he neglected this precaution. The rock broke away and went swinging down in a wide arc. With his weight on his arms, Bert scrambled for a new position and luckily found it. He had taken off his mittens, the better to feel the rock, and his finger tips were absorbing the chill of the rocks.

It seemed that hours had passed, but his watch confirmed that only minutes had gone by, when he planted both feet on the ledge and called up, "Okay, I've made it!"

"Good," came down Holliday's voice, oddly magnified by an echo from the surrounding cliffs. "Now move to one side so Ed can climb down. Don't want him to kick any rocks on your head."

As Holliday finished his words, Ed's boots and tapered ski trousers came over the top of the ledge. It took him only a few minutes to make the descent, and Bert felt a thrill of pride at his brother's sure-footedness. "Good old Ed!" he thought. "He's always careful, always precise, and just about always right."

Then Holliday's ironshod boots appeared against the skyline, and the ranger himself began to drop down toward them. The two boys looked at one another, and what they saw amused them both. Ed was first to laugh.

"Boy," he said to his brother, "you look like something the cat dragged in. Your face is all puffy, and your hair is standing right on end!"

"Well, Ed, I don't think the cat would even bother to

drag *you* in," Bert chuckled. " You look as if you hadn't slept for a month."

Bert looked over his shoulder at the valley floor. A lone car crawled up the road toward the Chalet, and a plume of smoke rose from the Wallace cabin.

"We're getting down fast," he said, "and I guess we'd better keep on hurrying." He jerked his tousled head toward the thickening sky.

"We'll make it all right," said Holliday, shielding his eyes against the haze as he looked out across the valley.

A faint mist seemed to sweep across the lower cliffs as Bert, his brother and the ranger dropped down toward the valley floor.

By now Bert was beginning to feel confident of his newly discovered skill as a climber. He frolicked down the cliffs with the assurance of a veteran. Places that had troubled him on the upward climb were no bother at all going down. His speed drew a warning from Holliday when all three members of the party assembled on the last steep cliff above the gravel slopes and highway.

"This is a tough place," the ranger cautioned him. "The rock is loose. Take it easy."

"Aw, I won't have any trouble," said Bert cockily, and

scrambled out over the edge of the rock. He was working down through a crack, swiftly as usual, when it happened. A chunk of rock beneath his feet slipped out and disappeared soundlessly into space. A projecting sliver to which he was holding with his right hand broke away with a sharp crack. Before he knew it, he was hanging on for dear life with his left hand. And his left hand was getting tired.

"You all right?" came the call from above.

"Sure," Bert said hoarsely. As he said the word, his numbed left hand gave away, and he dropped out into space. It all happened so quickly, as he said later, that he had no time to say anything. He dropped a foot—sixteen inches and then he came to a stop, slowly spinning in mid-air, with the rope tight around his chest.

"You're all right," came Holliday's voice. "I've got you solidly. Just let me lower you a little bit until you can get your feet on the rock again."

Bert, helpless, felt himself drop down until his shoes touched the rock. He grabbed for handholds and then stood firmly on a little ledge, breathing deeply.

"Okay," he called up. "I'll rest a minute and then keep on going down."

The gravel slope was not far beneath him, and Bert shakily made his way down to it. Then for the first time he drew a really deep breath and sat down. He was trembling. He looked gratefully out at the valley floor, now so close by, and tried to relax. Finally he felt a hand on his shoulder and glanced up at the ranger.

"Don't let it scare you," said the ranger. Bert could feel the reassurance in his voice. "Things like that happen to every climber. Just remember. Test every foothold and handhold when you're climbing. If they don't seem secure, and you're supported by a rope, call up to the fellow who's holding you and tell him to tighten the rope. I could have saved you that fall if you'd let me know."

Bert nodded his head. "I get it now," he said. "I guess I'll just have to be a little more careful."

"Be like your brother," the ranger added. "He's always cautious. You follow his example, and you'll never get into trouble."

"Okay," Bert said cheerily, a smile flickering across his troubled face. He got to his feet. "Anything below but scree?" he asked. The ranger shook his head.

"Then let's go!" Bert yelled and took off at a run down the gravel slope. At the bottom, panting and laughing, he stopped and untied the climbing rope.

"I feel as if I'd been away a million years," he said with sudden soberness.

"But it's only been twenty-four hours," Ed remarked quietly. "And now to get some food!"

Stumbling a little and feeling the relief from tension that had gripped them both, the brothers took off down the path to the highway from the ranger's cabin and plodded up the road to the Chalet. In the living room Mary Sue and Betty were sitting on a bench, chatting animatedly. They looked up as the brothers strolled in, and got to their feet.

"Where *have* you been?" the girls chorused. "You gave everybody a fright!"

"Oh, we decided to spend the night out," Bert said nonchalantly. "It was a little too warm down in the valley, and we thought we might be cooler up in the mountains."

"Well, come and have some breakfast," said Mary Sue. "You certainly must need it. Your brother has eaten already and gone back to bed. He was worried about you, too, and I guess it slowed up his recovery.

"Food?" asked Bert, attempting to sound incredulous. "Real food? Lead me to it, girls!" He sprinted for the dining room.

About fifteen pancakes and five glasses of milk later Bert finally leaned back with a luxurious sigh, wiped his lips, and said, "Well, now all I need is a little sleep, and I'll be all set."

"Me too," echoed his brother. "I'm really groggy. If you girls will excuse us—"

They rose stiffly from the breakfast table and walked from the dining room. Bert lingered at the desk in the lobby to inquire about mail.

"Just one letter," said the clerk, reaching into a pigeon-hole marked "Walton." He pulled out a long, very official-looking typewritten envelope. It was addressed to Bert, and in one corner was the ominous phrase: "Personal and confidential." The postmark, as Bert noted, was from Salt Lake City.

Bert quickly ripped open the envelope and took out the sheet of paper inside. It, also, was typewritten and unsigned. The message made him catch his breath and drop into a chair.

"If you want to find out exactly where your gold mine is located," read the message, "come to Castle Rock at 3 P.M. Tuesday. Bring your map. Friends will be there, and they will help you in your search. But come alone!" The last three words were underlined.

Bert scratched his head and looked up at the large calendar hanging on the wall. "Tuesday," he said to himself. "Holy smoke! This is Tuesday, and I'm dead for sleep." He took one decisive step toward the stairway to the bunkroom, then wheeled and strode across the living room to the steps that led down to the locker room.

Just as his head came level with the floor, he glanced upward and saw Alan strolling into the living room. Was that a smile on Alan's face? he wondered. Or was it just a wry grin?

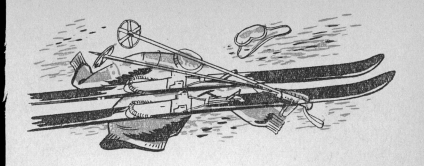

14   *Lost in the Blizzard*

The sky was a dull gray overhead, and the pinnacles of Castle Rock were almost invisible in the mists at the head of the valley. Bert paused for a moment, skis on his shoulders, as he walked out into the open air. The ski lift clanked upward and disappeared into a haze. On the peaks beyond, the snowstorm already was raging.

"I wonder if I ought to do it," Bert mused aloud. He took a quick look at his watch. It was eleven o'clock, and from the map on the waxing-room wall, he had seen that Castle Rock was at least four miles from the Chalet. He was troubled, too, because he hadn't told Ed or Howard. With a quick motion he set the skis in the snow and turned toward the door. Then he shook his head and turned away.

"Why bother?" he asked himself. "If I told them, they'd only try to discourage me. Anyway, I'll bet they're both asleep, and I don't want to wake 'em up." He shrugged his shoulders and bent over to fasten his skis. He slipped the straps of his ski poles over his mittened wrists and turned his face toward Castle Rock.

Inside his checked shirt he could feel the crinkled folds of Uncle John's map. He slid swiftly downhill to the brook and struck upstream along its banks, following an old pair of ski tracks. Here his skis ran smoothly, but a mile up the brook the tracks turned off to the left, and he was obliged to make his own route. Gray clouds lowered over the peaks to his right, and an occasional flake fell swiftly out of the sky and melted on the arms of his parka.

The skis were beginning to stick, and soon Bert was wallowing along almost as clumsily as if he had been afoot. Grumbling impatiently, he finally stopped, trod down a place in the snow beside a pine tree, and took off the skis. Using the metal tip of a ski pole, he scraped the snow loose and then reached in his pocket for his knife. With the opened blade he scraped off the last remnants of snow and methodically began to rub down the wax with the heel of his hand. Finally he extracted a chunk of paraffin from his pocket and rubbed it briskly across the soles of the skis. He knew very well what had happened. The temperature was rising, and the new-fallen snow was sticky.

With one last brisk rub he smoothed down the surface of the skis and slid them across the snow, making sure they would run freely before he finally bent down to put them on again. He had taken off his mittens, and now that he was finished, he looked around for them. The left mitten was visible, half-covered by the snowflakes that were falling faster and faster. But where was the right-hand mitten? He frantically dug with his ski pole at one or two suspicious-looking depressions in the snow. Finally he took the skis off again and began to excavate the dully glistening drifts.

"No use," he finally said to himself. "That mitten is gone —buried. I'll just have to get along without it and hope that it doesn't get any colder." But deep in his heart he knew that it probably would get colder before the storm was over. It always did, at least in New England, and he had no reason to think that things would be different here.

By now the snow was swirling and dancing before his eyes, but Bert simply pulled down his visor and trudged grimly on.

Wrrrr! There was an explosion in the snow just ahead of his ski tip. For a moment Bert's heart stopped dead. Something burst from the drifts and went rocketing off into gray space. He took another step forward. Wrrr! A second explosion. This time Bert could see what it was, a ruffed grouse, nesting in the snow to keep warm. The old farmers back East used to talk about these birds, but he never before had seen one.

He bent his head and plowed on into the storm. The wind was rising imperceptibly, and in the pines it was making a faint, whistling sound. He could see through the flying snow how the treetops were gently waving, and for a moment the impulse to turn back was so powerful that it overpowered his determination to go on. He swung his body in the direction of the Chalet, but the hesitation was only a momentary one, and he promptly turned toward Castle Rock again.

The valley floor had steepened now, and he was climbing uphill. Great boulders reared up in his path now and then, and he was beginning to perspire from the exertion.

"Whew!" he whistled, and stopped in the shelter of a mammoth boulder. He took off his ski pole straps and stuck the poles in a drift a foot away. Then he stripped off his parka and tied it around his waist. He knew that he would be warm as long as he was climbing, but as soon as he got to the top and stopped, he would begin to chill. He grasped his bare right hand in his mittened left hand and rubbed it vigorously to restore the circulation. It might have been his imagination, but he fancied somehow that it was getting colder.

Ahead of him the wind was screaming shrilly around an obstacle. Now and then the sound stopped for a minute and he could hear the thudding of his heart. It was only for a minute, however. Each time, the wind seemed to gather renewed force, and he could hear the great trees off on the hillsides as they groaned and cracked.

The white slope seemed to stretch on endlessly, but Bert kept plodding upward. He knew, he was sure, that Castle Rock must be at the top of it. A great gray pinnacle of rock rose up in front of him, and he automatically started around to the right of it. Only, as he saw, it was a long way around. And suddenly he realized that he had arrived at Castle Rock.

"But it's such a big place!" he remarked to himself. "How can I ever find anyone up here?"

The urge to get out of the wind hurried him onward, and Bert soon found himself in a small cranny between a mammoth pine and the edge of the rock, where he could sit quietly, half-leaning against the rock, with his skis on.

Out in front of him he could see the storm clouds whisking
by. The wind seemed to be trying to outdo itself. It rose
to one final screech, and then for a moment there was complete silence. As the snow drifted noiselessly down, Bert
caught the sound of voices off to his left. A grin split his
face, and he slid quickly along the wall, half carried by
another gust of wind. Then there was silence again, and
he could hear the voices clearly:

"You grab the kid and get the map away from him.
We can 'lose' one of his skis and let him stay out here to
freeze." And then a short, sharp bark of laughter. Bert
leaned forward against a dead tree branch to hear more
of the conversation. If this was a trap, he reasoned, he had
better learn who was laying it before he sneaked away. The
wind rose to a screech again, and its violence covered the
snapping sound as the branch gave away. Bert found
himself diving forward across a slope.

"Hey!" yelled a hoarse voice. "Catch that kid!"

Off to his left, through the driving snow, Bert could see
a burly figure in a mackinaw and another, slighter figure
huddled close to a campfire. Then the hillside dropped
away and he was plummeting down toward the valley
floor. The shouting behind him died away. He had eluded

his pursuers. Now all he had to do was to get back to the Chalet.

In the brief interlude at Castle Rock the wind had changed and sharpened. Where it had screeched, it now roared. And back of its roar was a biting cold. Bert's ears began to tingle, and he pulled the flaps of his ski cap down over his head. His right hand began to feel numb. He stopped in the shelter of a pine tree and glanced down. Was he mistaken, or was his thumb beginning to turn white? He frantically massaged the hand until he could feel the blood hammering in it. With his back to the storm he pulled on his parka and thrust the half-frozen hand beneath it.

His watch said four forty. It would soon be dark, he realized. Maybe the best thing would be to camp out and build a fire. But the weariness in his bones told him no, and his good sense confirmed this judgment. Whoever was chasing him wouldn't give up so quickly, even in a storm. No, he would have to keep on going and try to get back to the Chalet. With his jaw grimly set he pushed out into the storm again.

There was a yellowish tinge to the snow by now, and it played tricks on the eyesight. Flat places, hills and gullies, all seemed the same to Bert. Often he stumbled and fell in the snow. Once or twice he was tempted to lie still and let the delicious feeling of sleep creep over him. But he knew what would happen if he yielded, and so each time he wearily rose to his skis and slid onward.

Once when he stopped, his skis were projecting over a ledge, and he hastily pulled himself backward out of danger. A little later he came to a long slope of snow. "Something is wrong," he thought to himself. "I don't remember this." He veered away, but a little later he came back to the same slope at a slightly less steep point.

"Oh, well," he said to himself and pushed off into space. The snow flew past him, and his tired knees absorbed the occasional bumps and gullies, working like the shock absorbers on a car. Ahead he could see nothing at all through the flying snow. At last the slope leveled off, and he began to slow up.

"Thank heavens," he started to say. Beneath him there was a sharp, crackling sound. Before his numbed mind could react, he was waist deep in water. He had been standing on a shelf of ice overhanging the brook!

The icy water numbed Bert's legs, and, awakened to the danger, he struggled frantically toward the shore. His skis scraped across the rocks and gravel on the bottom of the brook as he gradually climbed out of the water. With a final push of his ski poles he was able to lift himself clear and onto land again. His ski trousers clung clammily to his legs, and he was shivering uncontrollably.

"Ought to build a fire and warm myself," he said between chattering teeth. But nowhere in the white, swirling expanse could he see a tree or even a chunk of driftwood. There was nothing to do but to ski on in and to hope for the best. His legs were leaden, weary and cold as he struggled up the hillside and out onto flat ground again. His hand had ceased to hurt, and he did not even bother to look at it. All he could think of was the door of the Chalet swinging open, and the fire inside, and hot food—hot soup, and a steak, and a brimming glass of milk.

His head bumped sharply against an immovable object, and Bert thought dully to himself, "I must be getting numb, bumping into trees like this—" He automatically moved to one side, slid forward a step, and bumped his head again. He looked up. It was a wall, the wall of a building. His skis were sliding underneath the building, and his head was bumping it. He moved slowly to the right, and then he saw where he was. It was the base station of the lift, and the Chalet was only a hundred feet away.

That last hundred feet seemed the longest part of the trip. Bert could feel his skis cut through the new snow to the hard-packed base beneath, where hundreds of skis had traveled. The Chalet was still invisible, but he staggered forward, almost tripping over his ski poles. Then a door swung open, warm air rushed out, and someone in the doorway said, "Why, it's Bert! And he looks half dead!"

Bert could hear the scraping of ski boots and the sound of voices as he collapsed in the snow. He dimly sensed that someone was taking off his skis. Then strong arms lifted him up, and he was carried inside the building. He felt the bright glare of the living-room lights on his closed eyes and then the resilience of cushions as he was gently laid on a sofa.

Very, very slowly he opened his eyes. He could see Ed bending solicitously over him, and he could feel the chill of cold water on his frozen hand as someone sponged it.

"I guess—I guess I almost took one chance too many," he whispered through swollen lips to his older brother. Then he closed his eyes again, and, before he knew it, was asleep. He dimly felt that he had earned the right to sleep for a long, long time.

15   *A Decisive Meet*

"Ouch!" Bert said abruptly. He had just flexed his right hand, which was swathed in bandages, and realized that he had made a mistake. He rolled his head on the snowy white pillow and looked across at his brothers, both of whom were sitting up in bed.

"Hurts, doesn't it?" asked Ed, compassion reflected in his eyes.

"Oh, not too badly," said Bert, and propped a pillow behind himself with his left hand as he, too, rose to a sitting position. He took a quick look at his wrist watch and snorted in disgust when he realized that it had stopped.

"Well, it's time for *us* to get up," chirped Howard from his bunk, accenting the *us*. Bert took a disgusted look at his younger brother, whose eyes were twinkling.

"And what makes you think *I'm* not going to get up on

152

this fine, sunny day?" he inquired, not quite concealing the annoyance in his voice.

"Oh, you're a cripple today," Howard said brightly. "You're all tired out, and you need a rest."

"You bet he does," added Ed somewhat grimly. "And I'm going to see that he gets it, even if I have to miss the *slalom* and sit on his chest to keep him in bed."

"Did you say *slalom?*" Bert demanded. He flung out his right arm with what was intended to be an appealing gesture, but then winced again as the blood hammered into his swollen hand.

"Why, sure," Ed answered him. "They're having another guest *slalom,* and it's a shame you won't be able to race."

"What makes you think I can't race?" Bert said challengingly. His normally ruddy face was flushed, and his red hair bristled as he leaned forward.

"Well, how can you with a bum hand?" demanded Ed. "The doctor said it would take three days or more before it's back to normal."

Bert cast a disgusted look at the bandages that swathed his hand. "Is it really frozen?" he asked. "Feels a little tingly right now."

"Well, it just missed being badly frozen," Ed replied.

"The doctor bandaged it while you were sleeping last night, and he said he'd be back this morning to look at it again. While we're waiting for him, why don't you tell us what happened?"

"Aw, I made a fool out of myself again," Bert said, wrinkling his nose at the memory. "I got a funny note asking me to show up at Castle Rock, and—"

"And when you did?" A voice from the doorway interrupted him. He looked up to see the bulky figure of Muldrow Holliday leaning against the doorjamb regarding Bert with a quizzical look.

"Oh, hello," murmured Bert. "Did you hear the first part of what I had to say?"

Holliday nodded, shifted the straw on which he was chewing, and motioned for Bert to continue his story.

"Well, I got out there, and somebody tried to grab me, but I got away."

"And who do you think that somebody was?" asked the ranger, curiosity written on his face.

Bert mused a moment, and then lifted his head and said defiantly, "I don't care what the rest of you think, I still believe it was Mr. Wallace."

Ed burst into a laugh and did not stop until Bert stared

reprovingly at him. "I think you've got the old gentleman on your mind," Ed finally chuckled. "As a matter of fact, he was sitting around the Chalet for an hour before you came in. So I guess that disposes of *him*."

"Well, maybe," Muldrow Holliday said thoughtfully. "And maybe not."

"Why do you say that?" asked Bert, his curiosity aroused.

"Because he could have gotten in an hour ahead of you," the ranger said. "There is a branch highway in back of Castle Rock. He could have driven up there, parked his car, and then lit out for the Chalet here while you were skiing back. You didn't take the trouble to ask about roads off in that direction, did you?"

"Well, no," Bert said slowly. "But none showed on the map."

"And did you happen to look down in the corner to see when that map was printed?" pursued the ranger. "Because, if you had, you would have discovered that the map was printed in 1908. The road wasn't built until 1919."

"Good grief," sighed Bert, sinking back on his pillow. "Then I could have avoided most of that trip."

"That's right," said the ranger.

A tapping on the door interrupted him, and a be-spectacled young man with a black bag in his hand strolled casually inside, nodding to Holliday.

"And how's our patient this morning?" he asked Bert, who stared blankly at him. "Oh—I forgot. You were asleep when I bandaged your hand last night. I'm the doctor."

"And just the man I want to see," said Bert, rising to a sitting position again. "Doctor, there's a *slalom* race today, and I've *got* to run in it. You see, last week I was disqualified, and so this week I've got to win."

"Well, let's look at the hand this morning," observed the doctor, setting down his bag and briskly unwrapping the tape and bandages on Bert's hand. Bert looked curiously at the swollen mass of flesh that emerged. It was lobster red, and tiny blisters had begun to break out on the backs of the fingers.

"Looks messy, doesn't it?" said the doctor. "You just missed having a badly frozen hand, my boy. As it is, this hand won't be in usable shape for a while. But—" he paused, and Bert could see his eyes twinkling behind his spectacles— "but I'm a skier myself and I know how you feel. So I'll tape this hand so you can use it in the *slalom*." He paused again as Bert wriggled beneath the coverlet.

"There's only one qualification," the doctor said. "It would hurt like the dickens if you fell down, so you've got to promise me to run a no-fall race."

"That I will! That I will!" Bert said, the words tumbling out of his mouth.

As the doctor strolled out the door, stopping for a moment to chat with Holliday in the hallway, Bert swung himself out of bed. He swiftly realized that he would have to readjust himself to new methods of getting dressed, since only his left hand was completely useful. Somehow, under the approving eyes of his brothers, he made it and followed them down the stairs to the dining room.

Breakfast was another difficult problem, for ham and eggs were on the menu, and he had only his left hand to use for eating. Fortunately the waitress was sympathetic. She brought him the ham and eggs neatly sliced and hovered near by to make sure that everything was all right. Halfway through the meal Bert looked up from his plate to see a familiar figure in the doorway. It was Alan, dressed in gray ski trousers with a knife-edge crease and a flaming red sweater.

"Too bad you can't race, Walton," he drawled at Bert. "But maybe you'll be in better shape next week."

"Thanks for the good wishes, old man," Bert said sarcastically. "But as it happens, I *can* race. And this time I'll make sure not to miss any gates."

Alan shrugged, turned his back, and strolled off into the living room. Bert turned back to his meal.

He swiftly gulped the last of his milk and walked down to the waxing room. His skis were already on the table, and a familiar figure was bent over them. It was Holliday. He straightened up as Bert approached and nodded down at the skis.

"Put my special formula on 'em," he said. "They ought to be as fast as greased lightning."

"Gee, thanks," said Bert, and meant it.

He reached for the skis, but Holliday anticipated him. "I'll carry 'em outside," said the ranger. He picked up the skis, and Bert followed him out the door. It was a brilliantly sunny day. On the slope alongside the lift tiny figures were at work packing the snow.

Bert was not even allowed to fasten his own ski bindings. Holliday dropped to one knee and clicked them shut, then handed Bert his ski poles.

"Good luck," he said. "It's a tricky course, so be careful. I know it's tricky, because I set the flags myself."

Somehow, despite his aching hand, Bert felt supremely confident as he slid down the hill toward the lift station. The skis on his feet, the snow on the ground, the sun in the sky, and the red-blue-orange flags on the hillside all fitted together in a pattern that was very pleasurable. He slid to a stop at the base station, opening his skis in a snow-plow V and then sidestepped up to the chairs. A mackinawed worker helped him onto the lift, and another man helped him off. All of them wished him good luck.

Very carefully Bert skied down beside the flags, observing the rule that he must stay at least fifteen feet away from them.

"Looks okay!" he shouted to Holliday, who was standing near the finish. The ranger nodded approvingly and made a circular motion with one hand, denoting "good luck." Bert glanced at his watch. Plenty of time for a trial run down alongside the flags. He hastened to get in line for the lift, and, as he rode up through the air, stared intently at the flags again. He was memorizing them, as any good racer does. In this case it was well he had, for some of the flags were hidden behind clumps of trees, and a whole grouping of them was invisible under the brow of the hill.

"Here's your number bib," said a tall, gray-haired man

standing at the top of the lift. Bert glanced at it swiftly before slipping the bib over his head. The number was thirteen.

He grinned and winked at the official. "Lucky number —I hope," he said.

He let his skis slide away from him and drifted down alongside the course, making each turn exactly as if he were running against time inside the flags. He felt easy, relaxed, and somehow supremely confident. He swung to a smooth, curving stop at the bottom of the hill and was surprised to hear the sound of applause. His two brothers were standing a little distance away with Mary Sue and Betty.

"Looking sharp, boy!" he heard Ed call out. He lifted his crippled hand in acknowledgment and started to turn away before he realized that neither of his brothers was wearing a number bib. He made a swift kick turn and skied over beside them.

"Hey," he said, "where're your numbers? Race starts in ten minutes."

"I know," Howard answered him, "but we decided to make this a one-man show. You're representing the Walton family, bub."

Bert began to protest, but Ed cut him short. "Go on and win," his older brother said gruffly. "This is a race between you and Alan, and we're counting on you." Bert felt a pat on his back, almost a shove, and he automatically slid away toward the lift.

At the top of the lift he noticed Alan just ahead of him. On his enemy's back the number bib bore the figure 22. That, he thought to himself, was fine. *He* could run and then watch how Alan did from a point up the course.

"You're next," said the starter, motioning him into position. Using his unharmed left hand, Bert balanced himself in position until the familiar ritual had been intoned, and he was on his way down the race course. He took the upper gates wide open; he stemmed just a little through the stem corridor, and he danced through a three-gate flush where he had to execute three quick turns. He felt fine, and he knew—as every skier does in moments of good skiing—that he was doing fine.

On the H his turns were exactly right. Bobbing and weaving, he shaved the corners, hopped through one more flush and a hairpin, and then crouched deep, his poles held out behind him to lessen wind resistance, as he flashed down through the finish flags. A minute later, as he relaxed, his time boomed out through the loud speakers: "Six seconds less than any of the other runners . . . the best time so far." He could feel his brothers pounding him on the back, but his eyes were fixed on the race course. He watched the next three runners come through, all of them slower than he was, before he started for the lift.

Alan was standing in the ready line as he reached the top. Tom Wallace's son ignored the nod Bert threw at him and turned his back. Bert shrugged his shoulders and then swung down leisurely to the midpoint of the *slalom* course, just above the H. From that point, he reminded himself, he could see most of the race. He watched numbers 19, 20 and 21 come through with varying degrees of speed, and then fastened his eyes on the hill above. That dark blob was Alan. Without envy and with appreciation for good skiing technique, he watched as Alan swung down powerfully through the first sequences of gates. In the stem corridor Alan took it straight, and Bert thought to himself, "It's fine, if he can hold the speed."

His rival was opposite him now and going like the wind. Just ahead was the H. Bert held his breath. Alan did not bother to turn. He simply swung his shoulders around to clear the flags and went skimming down through the narrow gate. And then, as Bert stared after him, he over-shot the next gate and took a walloping spill.

"Hurry up!" Bert shouted involuntarily. "You can still make it. You've been running in faster time than anyone else."

He could see the tanned oval of Alan's face turned up at him, and then he caught the disgusted gesture as Alan dropped one arm, planted his poles behind him, and skied off the course.

"Did not finish," broke in the loudspeaker. There was a disapproving note in the announcer's voice.

Bert felt a little sickened. The cardinal crime of a ski race was not to finish. He skied on to the bottom, ignoring other runners.

The last racer came through the flags as Bert reached the bottom of the hill. The timers went into a huddle, and the starter came skiing down from the top of the racecourse. Bert stood off at one side and chatted briefly with Mary Sue. All the time his mind was on the timers, busy with their pencils.

The loud sound of somebody's throat being cleared came over the loudspeaker system, and Bert involuntarily tensed his muscles.

"The winner," said the announcer, "is that fine sportsman, Bert Walton."

He had more to say, but Bert did not hear it. Suddenly people were pumping his uninjured left hand, slapping his back, and shouting congratulations. Finally somebody pinned a golden ski on his parka.

"That's for winning the race," said a voice, the voice of the chief timekeeper. "You did a fine job, Walton, and we're all very much pleased with you."

Bert blushed and stammered an acknowledgment. He shook hands and turned away. As he did so, he bumped into a towering figure. It was the doctor.

"Nice work, boy," said the doctor. "I guess that bandage worked all right."

"All right?" echoed Bert. "You bet it did! I feel as if the hand were healed already!"

16   *A Warning*

"Boy, I'm dying for a drink of milk," Bert confided to his brothers as they snapped loose their ski bindings in front of the waxing room.

"Want me to get it?" Howard asked Bert eagerly.

"No thanks, kid," he replied. "Just carry my skis in for me, and I'll run upstairs and see if I can persuade the cook to give me a glassful."

Leaving his brothers behind, he strode across the concrete floor of the waxing room and ran purposefully up the steps to the living room. At the doorway he hesitated in surprise. Mr. Wallace was standing there, talking to Alan!

For a moment Bert didn't know whether to turn back or to walk on into the room. He chose the latter course, but the two barely glanced at him as he passed.

"Oh, well," he said to himself. "Let sleeping dogs lie."

He gave the kitchen door a shove with his shoulder and found himself confronting the cook.

"Could I—could I have a glass of milk?" he asked. He could see a storm gathering on the chef's face, and he hastily added, "I just got through racing, and I'm dying of thirst." He watched the cook's eyes travel down to his injured hand, and then the white-hatted chef nodded his head.

"Sure, kid," he said. "I guess you're the young fella who won the *slalom*."

"That's right," said Bert, blushing a little. The cook snapped open the refrigerator door and wordlessly handed him a bottle of milk, followed by a glass.

"Thanks a lot!" said Bert gratefully and grabbed the bottle in his left hand.

He tipped the bottle up and began to pour. As the white fluid spilled into the glass, he glanced idly out through a window. His hand stiffened on the bottle. "Gravy!" he said to himself.

"Hey!" said the cook. "It's spillin' over."

"Sorry," said Bert, glancing down at the brimming glass and the widening puddle of milk on the porcelain table top. "Excuse me, I've got business outside."

He dashed for the door, shoved it open with his left

shoulder, and sprinted around the corner. The bent and ragged back of an obviously old man was moving away. Bert thrust out his hand and gripped the man's shoulder.

"Hold up there, Willis King!" he said sharply. The huddle of rags squirmed in his grip. A grizzled face looked up at him. It was the mad prospector!

"Where've you been, King?" Bert demanded. "All sorts of strange things have been happening around here, and I want you to tell me what you had to do with them!"

The prospector squirmed and tried to pull away. In a whining voice he said, "You let me go, Bert Walton! I ain't done nuthin'—and I got nuthin' to talk to you about!"

"Nothing!" burst out the astounded Bert. "Do you call that episode up at Skeleton Cave nothing? Why, you tried to keep me a prisoner there! You haven't forgotten that!"

"I don't know what you're talkin' about," whined the prospector, looking blearily at Bert. A sly grin overspread his face. " 'Pears to me like you got a lively imagination, boy. I don't know no Skeleton Cave, and I don't know what you mean about my trying to keep you a prisoner."

Bert swallowed and squared his shoulders to suppress the mounting rage within him. Finally in a calmer voice he said, "You don't remember taking me up the mountain?"

"Of course I don't remember it!" said the prospector in a singsong voice. "The only times I ever seen you was right down here aside the Chalet. You must be dreamin', boy. You must be dreamin'."

Bert felt like holding his head. This nightmare conversation was getting him down. With an effort he calmed himself and asked one last question. "Well, aside from that, where have you been these last few days?"

The answer made him shake his head in disgust.

"Why, right around here," cackled the prospector.

Bert released the mad prospector and gave him a shove.

"All right," he said hoarsely. "Go on then. But we'll catch up with you some one of these days, Willis King. And when we do, you may have to prove to the police that you're crazy. That is, if you are."

The wizened prospector scuttled away, his head still bent, but his shoulders shaking as if with secret mirth. Bert went back to the kitchen and drank his glass of milk. He remembered to thank the cook and then walked out into the living room. As he had suspected, Tom Wallace had vanished. Alan, sitting in a chair beside the fireplace, looked up and gave him a baleful glare.

Head down, Bert plodded across the room and slowly

walked upstairs to the bunkroom.

Moments later Ed and Howard strolled in through the door, satisfied grins on their faces.

"Come on, cheer up and look like the successful winner of a *slalom* race!" Ed observed, patting him on the shoulder.

Bert told them of his discovery that the mad prospector had returned, and described his strange conversation.

"Well, just let things run along," cautioned Ed, "and perhaps everything will work out. We should be hearing from Mr. Wilson. Maybe he'll have some clues for us."

"Yeah," piped up Howard, "and, besides, this is a day to celebrate. There's going to be a big masquerade party tonight, and we've got to rig up some costumes."

"You rig 'em up," said Bert, suppressing a yawn. "I'm tired. I'm going to doze awhile, and then I'll think about the masquerade." He leaned back against the pillow and dropped off to sleep.

The sound of the dinner bell and the rumble of voices from the living room woke him. He went to the washbasin, scrubbed his face, and ran a comb through his stubborn hair before starting downstairs. In the living room a cluster of guests was gathered around a huge sheet of brown paper that hung from the ceiling to the floor.

Chalet Gazette, said the heading. Beneath were news headlines—one of them about his victory in the *slalom*—plus hand-lettered "news articles," caricatures, and little poems. Every guest had been mentioned, and every one had been treated kindly.

"Who did it?" Bert inquired. An older man, whose name he did not know, turned around and said, "Why, Mary Sue and Betty. Mighty clever, isn't it?"

"You bet!" said Bert, glancing down at a caricature that obviously was intended to represent his face. The caricature had flaming red hair, carefully sketched in with a crayon, a wide smile, and this little poem beneath:

> Down the hills our Bert does fly,
> Like a rocket plane;
> Judging from the speed he shows,
> He'll finish up in Maine!

Bert joined in the general laughter as the other guests read the poem aloud and then strolled on into the dining room. His brothers looked up at him as he entered. They were sitting at a side table, deep in conversation.

"We've got a costume for you!" they said. "You're going as a prospector!"

"But what are you going to use for clothes?" Bert asked. The boys reached down and pulled out a battered pair of high boots, a pair of baggy denim pants, and a checked shirt, plus a wide-brimmed straw hat.

"We got 'em from the mayor," they said. "All you need now is a pick, and we're getting that from the kitchen crew. They keep one outside the back door to chop away the snow as it accumulates. We've even made a mask for you."

"Well, okay," Bert said doubtfully. "But what're you going to do about my red hair?"

His brothers exchanged glances. Then Howard chuckled. "Why didn't I think of it before?" he asked Ed, who was bursting with curiosity. "We'll use an old mop." He slid out from his chair, sprinted to the kitchen, and returned a moment later with a stringy mop, which had been detached from its handle.

"That does it," he said, flinging the mop at Bert, who had already gathered up the rest of his costume. "Drop it in the bunkroom, and come down. We're having an early dinner."

The strains of radio music were filling the Chalet when Bert, dressed in his prospector's costume, finally scuffed down the hall in his oversize boots and began his slow descent to the living room. He looked in through the door to see couples dancing—a girl in ballet costume, men in every conceivable sort of costume they could invent on the spur of the moment. He looked for his brothers, but he could not identify them. They had declined to change into costume while he was in the bunkroom.

The crowd filled the room, and Bert edged his way along the wall until he stood directly alongside the *Chalet News*. While waiting for the music to stop so that he could choose a dancing partner, he turned round and idly looked at the news items on the brown paper. Something had been pasted over the poem beneath his caricature, he noted. He bent down to look at it, and a chill went through his body. The new addition to the *Chalet News* was not a poem. It was a warning.

"Lay off, Bert," it said in block letters. "Lay off, or you'll get yourself in bad trouble. You have been warned!"

Bert rose to his full height and swung around to see if anyone were watching him. The dancers were absorbed in the music. He edged along until his left hand touched the pasted-in warning. He ripped it loose and stuffed it into his pocket. As the music stopped, he moved out on the floor and claimed the girl in the ballet skirt.

17   *A Stranger Comes to Call*

"Well, I don't see who could have done it but old Mr. Wallace," Bert said stubbornly. "Who else would have a motive?"

He scuffed his toe on the worn rug and looked up challengingly at his brothers. Howard was lying back on his bunk, whistling abstractedly and not seeming to be paying much attention to the conversation. Ed's serious face was wrinkled in a puzzled frown.

"Everything seems to point to the Wallaces," Bert repeated. "And when we hear from Mr. Wilson again, I'm going to tell him so."

"Yeah, should be about time for him to be visiting us again," Ed remarked.

"Well, I think I'll wax my skis," said Howard. He grunted as he rose up from his pillow and swung his feet down from the bunk. The grunt was replaced by a cry of "Ouch!" Bert looked up, an inquiring expression on his face.

"It's that doggone hunk of fool's gold," said Howard, grimacing and pointing to the rock Bert had so carefully brought down from Skeleton Cave. "I gave my ankle an awful bang." He picked up the chunk and drew back his hand, as if to throw it through the open window.

"Don't do that!" said Bert sharply. "I want it as a souvenir." He reached forward and took the rock away from his younger brother, using his bandaged right hand. Most of the swelling in the hand had vanished overnight, and a peek beneath the bandages had given him hope that in another day he could remove them entirely.

"Matter of fact," he said to Howard as a sudden thought struck him, "why don't you do me a favor? Get a box and some wrapping paper, and we'll mail this home. It'll be easier than carrying it back in a suitcase."

Howard nodded and went whistling out the door. Bert looked after him, amusement written on his face. "Cheerful kid," he said, and Ed nodded agreement. A moment later he heard scuffling and the same tuneless whistling. Howard poked his head back through the door.

In his right hand was a small cardboard box, in his left,

a piece of brown wrapping paper and some string that trailed forlornly down to the floor.

"I guess you'd better put on the address, Howie," said Bert, reaching for a fountain pen on the window sill at the head of his bunk. "Just address it to Dad, and I'll add a little note. None of your usual scrawl either. Let's see if you can't print legibly."

Howard pulled a suitcase from beneath his own bunk, and, using it as a writing table, spread out the brown paper and began to print Mr. Walton's address in large, black letters. Bert rose to his feet and strolled over, watching idly as the first words of the address took shape. Suddenly he narrowed his eyes.

"Give me that paper!" he said sharply and yanked it away from Howard. The pen left a long, scratchy line on the paper, but Bert paid no attention to that. He sat down abruptly, scrutinized the lettering, and then looked accusingly at Howard.

"You bum!" he said. "Now I know who printed that warning sign last night. You printed it!"

"Why, how can you say such a thing?" Howard asked. He tried to assume a hurt tone of voice, but he didn't succeed very well.

Bert reached in his left hip pocket with his uninjured hand, pulled out the warning notice and laid it on the wrapping paper. With his bandaged fist he pointed at the two pieces of printing.

"Look here," he said. "Same lettering exactly." His mouth flew open as he noticed something else. He snatched up the warning notice and fitted it into a torn corner of the larger piece of paper.

"Fits perfectly," he said. "Sherlock Holmes has solved the mystery."

Howard doubled up with laughter. "You've been so deadly serious about everything lately that I thought I'd just add a little more to the mystery," he finally said. "I was going to tell you a little later on, but it was too good a joke to resist at the time."

"I ought to paddle you!" Bert said sharply, but the vexed note in his voice was dwindling, and he finally broke down and began to laugh. "Well, I guess maybe I *have* been too suspicious," he confessed. "And maybe some of the things that happened were accidental, when I thought they were done on purpose. But I still think most were planned."

"And not by me," Howard interrupted. "Honest to Pete, that warning note I stuck on the wall last night was the first and last joke I've played."

"Anyway," Ed added judicially, "don't jump at conclusions about the Wallaces, or about anyone else, until you've had a chance to talk to Mr. Wilson. He's a lawyer, just like Dad, and he'll be better able to judge than we are."

"Okay," Bert agreed. "We'll let things stay as they are until we see Mr. Wilson. Now let's wax our skis and get going. The lift must be running by now."

"Is this a good day for skiing!" yelled Howard as he went out the door. "Perfect powder snow and lots of sunshine! We need only one more day of sun to be just about as tanned as a tribe of Indians!"

Bert heard his younger brother's footsteps echoing down the hall as he laced his own boots and strolled more slowly out the door, followed by Ed. But he took the steps to the living room two at a time and burst out through the archway. As he spun into the living room, he narrowly escaped a collision with a dapper young man whose gray business suit seemed oddly out of place in a lodge for skiers.

"Oh, excuse me!" he panted.

The young man gave him a sleek grin, displaying all his gleaming white teeth, and said, "Oh, that's all right, young man. As long as you missed me there's nothing to apologize

for. By chance do you know if Bert Walton or his brothers
are here? I have a message for them from Mr. Wilson, the
attorney."

"Why, I'm Bert Walton," Bert said grudgingly.

"My name is John Bates," said the stranger. He gave Bert
a flabby handshake. "Mr. Wilson asked me to stop by to
talk with you."

"Well—okay," Bert said slowly. "But I think my brothers
ought to be here."

He swung around and looked long and hard at Ed. His
brother's face wore its usual calm expression. Ed introduced
himself to the sleek-haired stranger with less reluctance
than had Bert.

"I'll go get Howie," said Bert. He walked over to the
stairway leading to the waxing room and let out a shout.

"Okay, okay, I'm coming." A voice floated up to him,
and he could hear Howard's heavy tread on the stairs. In a
moment his brother burst into the room.

"What's the idea—" Howard started to say and then
broke off abruptly as he looked at the stranger.

"This is Mr. John Bates," Bert told him. "Mr. Wilson
couldn't come up the mountain today, so he sent this
gentleman instead."

"It's nice of you to make the trip," Howard said gratefully. "Let's sit down." He plunked himself on a sofa. Bates sat down gingerly, first pulling up his trouser legs so as not to mar the knife-edge crease that contributed to the impression he gave of being extremely fastidious.

"I'm not quite familiar with all the details," Bates remarked, pulling a cigarette from his vest pocket and lighting it with a gleaming lighter. "Perhaps you'd better start at the beginning and fill in for me."

"Let me tell it!" Howard said eagerly. "Bert, you've gone over the story so often you must be tired of telling it."

"Okay," Bert said wearily. "But don't make it too dramatic. While you're talking, I think I'll go out in the kitchen and get myself a drink of water."

He excused himself and started toward the kitchen. Somehow he felt vaguely uneasy about the whole thing.

As he pushed open the swinging door to the kitchen, the first thing on which his roving eye alighted was the figure of Alan, slouched in a chair beside the table, chatting animatedly with the cook.

"Oh, hello," he said nonchalantly and apologized for interrupting. Ignoring Alan, he walked over to the sink, turned on the tap, and reached for a glass. When it was filled with cool, clear water, he turned off the tap and swallowed the water with his back toward his rival.

"Oh, you don't need to be so exclusive," a sneering voice taunted him. "Just because you won the *slalom,* there's no need to think that you're the king bee around here."

"Now, wait a minute—" Bert began. Alan wouldn't let him finish the sentence.

"You're a bright young fellow, Bert," he said in a drawling voice. "Too bright, perhaps. I won't go into details about that. But no matter what anybody else says, I think you're stuck-up and swell-headed."

Bert clenched his fists, but swallowed his anger before replying.

"I don't want to argue with you, Alan," he said in a quiet but tense voice. "Just cut out talking that way. I'm here to have a good time, and there's no reason for any jealousy between us."

"Aah, go peddle your papers somewhere else!" Alan snarled. He got to his feet with lazy insolence and walked toward the back door.

"Don't mind him, kid," the cook said by way of consolation. "He's always got a chip on his shoulder. Just like his dad that way, I might tell you."

"Well, I don't want to fight with anybody," said Bert, the anger in his voice ebbing slowly away, "but he's certainly asking for trouble."

He stalked across the kitchen and swung open the door to the dining room. He could hear Howard's sharp, quick voice. "—and then the old prospector tried to keep Bert a prisoner up there in Skeleton Cave, but my brother was too smart for him. He got away."

"Don't build me up so much, Howard," Bert chided his brother as he came back into the living room. "I just ran because I was scared to stay in the cave with that old fellow."

An unctuous smile came over Mr. Bates's face as he listened to Howard's explanation.

"Well, some people say that old Willis King is crazy," he remarked, "but I think he's crazy as a fox—in other words, a lot more sane than you'd believe. I'd be willing to bet you that all the trouble you've been having can be traced back to Willis King. He thinks you're trying to cheat him out of his gold. Of course, he hasn't any gold. There isn't any up here any more."

"Then you don't believe that Uncle John's mine is worth looking for?" asked Bert. Somewhere back in his mind a danger signal was sounding.

"Of course not!" said Bates, looking intently at Bert. "This country has been thoroughly prospected for gold, and it's a cinch that there's none to be found, at least in this canyon. Why, hundreds of men have combed these hills."

Bert stole a glance at his brothers. Ed looker sober and reflective. Howard's face wore a crestfallen look.

"But just out of curiosity, why don't you let me look at your map," Bates continued. "I know this country about as well as Mr. Wilson, and it'll be interesting to see what this particular map looks like."

"I'll have to go upstairs to get it," Bert said. Was he wrong, or did a sudden light leap into Mr. Bates's dark eyes as he moved to get up?

"Okay, I'll wait," said Bates. He relaxed and lit another cigarette, then began to chat with Ed and Howard about skiing. Bert walked to the door and stood there a minute, looking back at his brothers.

At the top of the stairs he stopped, puzzled. Just what could he do to stall off Bates for a few minutes? And just how could he confirm his suspicions? The only telephone was downstairs, unless— He walked to the end of the hall and tapped on a door that said "Private." A voice from inside called, "Come in."

Bert swung open the door and confronted a gray-haired man who was sitting idly in an easy chair listening to the soft music of a radio.

"Excuse me," he stammered. "Are you the manager?"

"That's right," the gray-haired man answered him. "And I suppose you're Bert Walton. I've been away, as you probably know, and I just got back from the city this afternoon. And now, what can I do for you?"

"Well, I thought you might have a telephone connected to the switchboard downstairs," Bert said hesitantly. "I've got a confidential, long-distance call to make, and I can't very well use the public phone in the living room."

The gray-haired man raised his eyebrows. "Very well," he said, gesturing toward a telephone on the desk beside the radio. "Go ahead and use my phone."

"Thanks," said Bert gratefully. He lifted the receiver. "Hello," said the tinny voice of the clerk on duty at the desk downstairs.

"This is Bert Walton," Bert said in a low, confidential voice. "Please don't repeat my name. I've an urgent call to make to Mr. Robert Wilson in Salt Lake City. Can you get it for me, please?"

There was a buzzing and clicking on the line and then

the voice of the switchboard operator repeating the call to another operator in Salt Lake City, followed by the sound of buzzing again.

"Mr. Wilson's law office," said a feminine voice.

"Is Mr. Wilson there?" Bert asked breathlessly. "This is Bert Walton at Sunmount."

"Oh, yes, Mr. Walton," the voice replied. "I'll put him on."

There was a click, and Wilson's voice came clearly over the phone: "Yes, Bert?"

"Mr. Wilson, did you send a man named Bates up here to talk with us?" Bert asked.

"Bates? Is he there?" came the voice from the other end of the phone.

"Yes, and he wants to see the map," said Bert, still in the same low, confidential tone of voice. By now his heart was pumping faster. "Shall I show it to him?"

"Under no circumstances," Mr. Wilson said sternly. "I didn't send him up, and I don't know whom he's representing, but I'll tell you this. He's a lawyer who has been mixed up in a number of shady deals, and he's not to be trusted."

"Well, then what shall I do?" demanded Bert. "Shall I tell him I'm on to his game, or what?"

"Don't do that," said Mr. Wilson, speaking sharply. "Just treat him nicely, tell him good-by, and say that you've mislaid the map. Maybe we can fool him at his own game—lead him on, and find out who's hired him."

"Okay," Bert said soberly. "Thanks a lot, Mr. Wilson." He hung up. "Thanks," he said to the manager, who nodded acknowledgment. He walked out and carefully closed the door. From downstairs he could hear Mr. Bates's low, drawling voice and the voices of his brothers. He walked on into the living room.

"Gee, I'm sorry, sir," he said apologetically to Bates, who raised his eyes. "I just can't seem to locate that map right now. Guess I've mislaid it. Tell you what I'll do—I'll send it down to Mr. Wilson when I find it. How will that be?"

"No, send it to me," said Bates, rising to his feet. "I'll be handling this matter from now on. I'll call you tomorrow about it." A grin split his face—a forced grin, Bert thought to himself. Bates shook hands all around, swung into his overcoat, and disappeared through the door.

"Nice fellow," mused Howard, watching Bates vanish around the corner of the house.

"Nice fellow?" echoed Bert. "Nice crook, you mean. That man's a fraud."

18   *A Good Day for Skiing*

During the night there had been a light fall of snow.
Bert had awakened once in the early morning hours to hear
the wind whining around the Chalet, for all the world like
a dog that had been lost and was seeking shelter. He lay
drowsily listening to the sound for a moment and reflecting
on the joys of a warm bed as contrasted to the cold outside.
Then he dropped off into a heavy slumber again to dream
of all manner of things. The thread of his conversations
with Bates somehow wove itself into a wild fantasy of
snow, avalanches, and mine tunnels that had no ending.
At last he slept soundly. The next thing he heard was the
sound of the breakfast bell.

"Hurry, hurry, hurry!" chanted Howard, imitating a
circus barker. "This way to the big tent, folks. See the
dancing orange juice. Watch the bacon sizzle. Stick a fork

in the eggs and see how they scramble—" He broke off abruptly as Bert leaned out of bed, picked up a slipper and heaved it at him. Howard was just thrusting one leg into his ski trousers. He ducked, tumbling over on the floor.

"That's what you get for being so noisy, small fry," Bert growled and shied the other slipper at his young brother as he swung his feet out of bed, shivering a little when they touched the cold floor. He closed the window with a bang, and sparkling flakes of snow eddied into the room. Howard, grinning, tossed the slippers back to him and Bert put them on, shivering as he did so.

"Wow, it's cold," he said and clicked his teeth together in a none-too-convincing demonstration of how cold he was. By now the radiator was beginning to spread its warmth through the chilly room, and Bert continued dressing in a more leisurely fashion. As he sloshed water onto his face, blowing and puffing, he noticed Ed beside him.

"Let's hope this is one peaceful day," he said fervently to his older brother. "I'm tired of all this excitement."

"Well, if we stay on the lift and ski, I don't see what can happen," Ed replied. "At least, whatever does happen, we'll have to blame on ourselves."

"Righto," said Bert happily. "It's a perfect day for staying close to home. And by the way—" he paused for dramatic effect, "I've just been checking my pocketbook. Looks to me as if we have enough money for a ski lesson today."

"Well, I don't see why we need to take lessons," Howard broke in. "Don't we know just about all we need to about skiing? Seems to me we're doing pretty well."

Bert regarded him thoughtfully. "Don't ever say a thing like that," he warned Howard. "You *never* can know too much about skiing. And what's more, Pete Andersen, the instructor, is due back today, and he's one of the best all-around skiers in the West. We can learn a lot from him, and I certainly intend to."

"Well, okay," said Howard, but doubt still lingered in his voice. "Want me to go down now and sign up for ski tickets?" He edged warily toward the door and sprinted out as Bert nodded assent.

Bert cast an amused look at Ed, who shrugged his shoulders and held out his hands in an expressive gesture before remarking, "He'll know better after this lesson."

As they walked into the dining room, a blond, square-faced man in his thirties was sitting at a small table, talking earnestly to a pretty woman across from him.

"That's the ski teacher," whispered Howard, as Bert and

Ed sat down beside him. "He's sure a husky fellow."

"Sure is," agreed Bert, spooning up his steaming cereal. "He'd have to be husky to ski the way he does. I've seen him in the newsreels. Power? Boy!"

A little later, as Bert and his brothers were waxing their skis, Andersen strolled up to them. He put out a hamlike hand and said, "I guess you are the Walton boys. They tell me you are skiing with me this morning. Now, what would you like to work on?"

"Oh, we'll leave that up to you, Mr. Andersen," Bert said shyly.

"Well, let's do a little downhill running, and then how about some jumping?" asked the instructor. He patted a pair of jumping skis which lay on the waxing table alongside Bert's narrower skis.

"Why, sure, if you think we can do it," said Bert, who was a little doubtful about his own ability as a ski jumper.

"Of course you can," said the instructor, "and it'll help you in your downhill and *slalom* running. The boys and I built up a little jump, about a fifteen-meter one, on the hillside yesterday."

"What do you mean by a fifteen-meter jump?" asked Howard curiously.

"Well, that means that the maximum distance you can jump is about forty-five feet," said the instructor. "A meter is about three feet. But to start with, we'll jump shorter distances. Come, get ready now, and we'll go out."

Bert and his brothers followed the instructor through the door, put on their skis and slid down toward the lift, admiring Andersen's fluent, smooth way of skiing. He seemed completely relaxed; yet behind that relaxation they could sense great power, plus the ability to cope with any situation.

The blackboard on the lift platform was entirely free of any avalanche warnings, but it did contain one pleasing item of information. The upper lift, closed for repairs since the boys had arrived at Sunmount, was to be open at one p.m.

"And the snow will be ten feet deep up there!" exulted Bert, who had looked longingly at the upper hill for days, but never tried to ski on it because the lift wasn't functioning. It was a funny thing, he reflected, but skiers never like to climb uphill if there's any sort of transportation, such as a lift. And if the lift isn't running, they stay on the flat.

He was musing so deeply on this paradox that it took him a moment to realize that a whole procession of empty chairs had clicked by him. Andersen and his brothers were already halfway up the hill. He hastily grabbed the next chair to come around and swung out into space. When he reached the summit, he saw the instructor, Ed and Howard skiing across the hill and out into the deep snow toward the Plummet Run. Always before, Plummet had been closed because of avalanche danger. Today it was open for the first time. Bert put on a burst of speed and dove into the deep snow to catch up with the others. He found them standing at the top of a steep pitch, which was punctuated by pine trees barely poking their heads above the snow.

"Now, the thing I want you to remember," Andersen said seriously to the three boys, "is that your turns in deep snow should be evenly spaced, smooth and regular. If your ski tips begin to dive, just sit back a little. Make a smooth, round turn, and you'll have no trouble."

He dug in his ski poles and leaped over a tiny snow cornice, landing light as a feather in the drifts below. The snow here was so deep that Andersen was buried to his knees. Still he swung down, leaving a plume of fluff behind him, until finally he curved to a stop and yelled, "Come on!"

Bert felt a little nervous as he began his first turn. It was one thing to ski in deep snow where the skis were visible, but the idea of going down a hill where your skis were invisible didn't appeal to him. The turn was jerky, and he lurched and staggered, but remained upright. He gritted his teeth and literally dived into the second turn. He was amazed at how smoothly it came around. His success gave him assurance, and he swung down almost as smoothly as the instructor, coming to a stop alongside Andersen.

"Very good indeed," remarked the instructor. "Now let's see your brothers."

First Ed, then Howard, came swirling down the hill. Both of them made smooth, flowing turns. As Howard came to a stop, he announced, "I take it all back. This lesson is doing me a lot of good."

"And so will our jumping," said Andersen cheerfully. "Come over here with me."

He led the way to a hillside so steep that it seemed almost vertical. A wide track had been stamped out of the snow, and high above them Bert could see where snow had been piled to make a take-off for the ski jump. As the boys climbed up, Andersen reassured them, "On a little hill like this you can jump without regular jumping skis. On a bigger one, of course, you'd need them."

Bert gulped as he reached the top. "Little?" he said. "Why, I can't even see over the edge of the jump."

"And you don't need to," said Andersen reassuringly. "Put your poles in the snow. You won't need them. Crouch when you go down, keep your hands out in front, and just ride off the edge of the take-off. That will get you used to the speed."

The instructor dropped into a deep crouch, whistled down the take-off, and disappeared into space.

"Here goes nothing," Bert said hollowly, looking at his brothers for reassurance. He fitted his skis into the tracks already packed out, crouched, and started down the take-off. The trees on either side were whistling by him. Suddenly he was out in the air, flying like a bird toward the valley. He straightened a little, almost automatically, and then dropped into a crouch again as his skis hit the snow. He could see the bottom of the hill coming up toward him, and he could faintly hear Andersen shouting, "Turn, turn!" He missed his ski poles, but he swung his body automatically and skidded to a stop.

"That's really an experience!" he gasped as Andersen grinned at him. He moved out of the way and watched as his brothers, one after the other, came plummeting out into the air and down to an adequate landing. Howard sat back too far and almost spilled, but by a great effort he controlled his skis and swung to a stop. Andersen jerked his head toward the top of the hill, and the three boys side-stepped up behind him.

"Boy, that's real fun!" Bert said. "Just as much fun as downhill or *slalom*."

"You bet it is!" agreed Andersen. "Now—do you want to jump some more or ski downhill?"

"Jumping for me," said Bert stoutly, and his two brothers concurred when they reached the foot of the hill. The morning passed all too swiftly. Not until Andersen looked at his wrist watch did Bert think of the time. He hastily consulted his own timepiece.

"Time to eat," he said to his brothers. "And I'll race you in, cross-country. We'll climb up, get our poles, and then cut across the mountainside."

Lounging in an easy chair, Bert felt an almost overpowering desire to sleep, but the thought of skiing on untracked snow was stronger. Bert resolutely looked at his watch. It was ten of one. "Let's go," he said, nudging his drowsy brothers. They shook their heads sleepily, then rose groaning to their feet and followed him to the waxing room.

"Let's hurry to be the first in line," Bert said persuasively. He looped his ski poles over his wrist, gave a push, and slid down toward the lift.

"What's this?" he said in a surprised tone, staring at the blackboard. The notice had been altered. The words "one o'clock" had been scratched out, and "two o'clock" substituted. "Well, that's all right," he said to his brothers, who had come up and were reading over his shoulder. "We'll just go over on Plummet and ski again."

At the top of Plummet, Bert paused and looked thoughtfully downhill.

"Let's play follow the leader," he suggested. "I'll go first and you try to catch me." He dived over the edge and swung down toward the trees, followed by his brothers.

"Ho, you've got to do better than that!" he shouted. Tiring of his brothers' slow pace, he swung around and started for the base of the lift. Off to his left he could see two figures, black in the brilliant sunshine. They seemed to be watching him. They were a long distance away, but even so, he could recognize the bulky shape of Tom Wallace. And, of course, that was Alan with him. As he watched, squinting his eyes, Alan detached himself from his father's side and started for the lift. The two boys met at the foot of the ramp.

"Oh, hello," said Alan with unusual cordiality. "Going to ski the upper lift soon's it's open, I suppose?"

"Yeah, I guess so," Bert said in a voice that he hoped was appropriately cool. "You, too?"

"Guess so." Alan smirked. "Looks as if there's going to be a crowd, and they might get the hill packed down in a hurry."

Bert had an impulse to wait for his brothers, but Alan was standing close behind him, almost urging him on. He reluctantly dug in his ski poles and slid over to the base station of the upper lift. There was a crowd, as Alan had said.

"If you're smart, you'll pick one of those red chairs," Alan said, leaning forward to emphasize his words. "The green ones aren't so comfortable."

Bert started to move forward, but Alan slid around in front of him. "Sorry," said his rival, "but I've got to fix a binding. Wait a second and I'll move on."

Alan adjusted his binding and then moved forward. A green chair was just coming around the lift pylon. Ignoring his own advice, he sat in it. Bert reluctantly moved up and sat in the next chair, a red one. As the chair started up the cable, Alan turned around and gave him a long look, an expectant look.

The cable suddenly came to a stop, and Bert found himself suspended over space. Just ahead an ugly-looking outcrop of rock stuck out of the snow like a jagged fang, and Bert shivered as he looked at it. "I'd hate to fall on that," he thought to himself. The cable began to move again, and Bert rode smoothly upward.

Suddenly his forward motion stopped. Over his head he heard a grating, grinding sound, and then his chair began to slide backward. His heart leaped into his throat, and he looked downward at the ground, twenty feet below. He could see the rock outcropping as his chair gathered speed in its backward movement. The rock outcropping was coming closer, closer. He could hear the frightened shouts of the man on duty in the lift station.

"Well, here goes," Bert thought to himself. He leaned forward and fell into space. He was tense, awaiting the grinding shock as he hit the rock. Instead he lit, spluttering and gasping, in a deep, billowy snowdrift. Before he could untangle himself, two skiers had swung down to a point alongside him and were helping him to his feet. He looked downhill. The outcropping was just three feet below him.

"Thank goodness!" he said gratefully. "That was a close one! What happened?"

"The clamp that held your chair to the cable came loose," said one of the skiers. "For a minute we thought you couldn't make it. But you showed good sense and jumped just in time."

"Well, so many things have happened to me lately that I wouldn't be surprised if somebody deliberately loosened that clamp," Bert said as soon as he got his breath.

"Oh, no, son," said the tall man, obviously shocked. "It was just carelessness on somebody's part. We had a chair come loose once before."

"But didn't you check the lift carefully before you opened it?" asked Bert angrily.

"Well, yes," said the tall man, "we did. But I still think that the bolts somehow worked loose on this one chair. Who would want to play a trick like that on you anyway?"

"I could name several people, but I won't," Bert said grimly. He grabbed his ski poles and swung down to the lift station where his two brothers were waiting for him. There was an angry frown on his face and cold resolution in his eyes as he waited for Alan to come down.

19   *In the Wallace Cabin*

The lobby next morning was a forest of skis. Three blond and bronzed Scandinavians who had troubled Bert by their lack of interest in downhill skiing turned out to be Norwegians on hand for the big jumping tournament.

"And how about you boys?" boomed a hearty voice as Bert and his brothers dawdled over breakfast. "Going over to the canyon to jump, I suppose?"

Bert looked across the table at his brothers. "Well, I'm going to stay around here today," he said. "I don't feel up to tournament jumping."

Ed broke into the conversation Bert was holding with a tall, ruddy man, who later introduced himself as the manager of the jumping tournament. "I think Howie and I will go touring today," he said. "Thanks for the invitation, but we aren't tournament jumpers either."

"Well, you'll miss a good day's competition," said the tall man. "We've got some real champions, like these Norwegian boys and Alan Wallace. He's one of the best of the local crew." He raised his eyebrows meaningly, but even Bert, who could display a fiery temper on occasion, did not respond to the hint.

"Thanks just the same," he said politely. "Maybe if we come back next year, we'll be in shape to compete against the experts."

The tall man nodded understandingly and strolled across the room to talk with the Norwegians.

As he left Bert's table, Mary Sue and Betty walked in through the archway from the living room and headed straight for the Walton boys.

"Who's going touring today?" Mary Sue wanted to know. Bert, who had a mouthful of pancakes, gestured toward his two brothers.

"Sounds like a good idea," said Howard, moving over to make room for the girls on the narrow bench. "But where'll we go?"

"Oh, I think up into Lost Man's Basin," said Mary Sue, sipping her glass of orange juice.

"Lost Man's Basin?" asked Bert. "I hope that's just a

name, not a prophecy." Howard nodded and grinned.

"Oh, no," said Mary Sue. "It's a long tour, but a perfectly safe one, as long as we follow the route Mr. Holliday has laid out."

"Well, if it's so safe, where does this Lost Man name come from?" Bert wanted to know.

"Oh, that's from the old mining days," Mary Sue said airily. "Some prospector got lost up there, and they never found him."

"Let's hope that doesn't happen to you," Bert drawled. "If it does, I'll have to rename it 'Lost Brothers' Basin.' By the way, when'll you be back?"

"Oh, I reckon around four o'clock," said Mary Sue. "If we're not back by six, you can round up the bloodhounds and send out the posse."

Bert lifted his hand in a gesture of farewell as Howard, Ed and the two girls slid out from their places at the table and strolled into the living room, talking animatedly. He was pouring himself a second cup of steaming cocoa when a shadow fell across the tablecloth, and he looked up, surprised, to see the sheriff of Sunmount standing there.

"How's everything, son?" asked the sheriff genially. "Mind if I sit down?" He suited the action to the words, then pulled out his pipe, struck a big wooden match, and puffed briskly.

"Things are still happening," Bert said ruefully, "but we haven't found the mine yet." He quickly sketched for the sheriff his experience on the lift the day before. He noted that the older man's face grew grim and drawn as he talked.

"Well, might be an accident, might be a-purpose," said the sheriff. "Certainly a lot of funny things have been happenin' to you. But I don't see how you can pin any of 'em on anybody in particular. You may have your suspicions, but suspicions won't hold up in court."

"What do you think I ought to do now?" Bert asked, and he really wanted advice. "Seems to me I've got to find those old mining records."

The sheriff's right eyelid dropped in a noticeable wink.

"Well, son," he said, "I don't approve of pokin' around other folks' houses, but if you think somebody is doin' somethin' wrong or withholdin' information that you should properly have, I think we can stretch the law a little bit and figger that you're justified in makin' your own investigation. I'm not tellin' you to, mind you. I'm just thinkin' out loud."

With the pipe clenched between his teeth, the sheriff

pushed back the bench and rose slowly to his feet. "So long, son," he said cordially and strolled out of the room. Bert thoughtfully sipped his cocoa.

Ed and Howard were busy packing their rucksacks when Bert strolled into the bunkroom.

"Where in the dickens is my waxing cork?" Howard demanded frantically. His brothers shrugged their shoulders, and Howard got down on his hands and knees to peer under the bunk. "Ah," he said with a sigh. "Here it is." He hauled out a dust-covered block of cork and tossed it into the open mouth of his rucksack. From an opened drawer he pulled a sweater and an extra shirt.

"Fine," said Ed, looking over his shoulder. "But what about first-aid equipment?"

"Aw, we won't need that," Howard said carelessly. "It'll just make the load heavier, and I must have fifteen pounds in my pack by now."

"Better take it along," Ed said.

"That's a smart thing to do," Bert said approvingly, his hands on his hips. "I'm beginning to believe in safety first around here. Particularly—" he paused meaningfully— "with Alan Wallace missing."

"You never did meet up with him after that accident

yesterday, did you, Bert?" asked Howard.

"No," said Bert. "I waited patiently at the bottom of the lower lift for an hour, but I guess he sneaked home some other way. You notice that he wasn't in for dinner. Looks to me like a guilty conscience."

"Well, maybe," said Ed. "I'm still not entirely convinced. Howard, here, thinks that everything that happened can be explained away. That may be due to the fact that he's always playing tricks. You think nothing that's happened can be explained. My own guess is that part of the troubles we've had were accidents, and part of 'em were the result of somebody's interference."

He pulled tight the top of his rucksack, cinched the straps that wound around his ski boots, and flung the pack on his shoulder.

"Well, anyway," he said to Bert, "too bad you're missing the trip. We'll be back pretty early. Take things easy. You need a rest anyway."

With a wave of his hand Ed vanished through the door. Howard shouldered his own pack with a grunt, looped his thumbs through the straps that ran down on either side of his chest, and followed out the doorway with dragging steps. Bert could hear the sound of footsteps down the hall, and then the heavy clump-clump of ski boots descending the stairs. He sat down on the edge of his bunk, then pulled his feet up, lay back, and dozed.

In his dreams he suddenly felt a great and consuming thirst. He tossed drowsily from side to side, then finally opened his eyes and swung his feet to the floor. He walked quickly downstairs, through the sunlit dining room, and pushed open the kitchen door.

"Oh, hello," said the tall, dark-haired cook. "Just the fella I want to see."

"Well, maybe we can make a trade," said Bert. "I'm dying for a glass of milk. I'll swap you for whatever you want."

"I've got a crate of milk bottles up by the road, and I need someone to help carry 'em down," said the cook. "All my help's off this morning."

"Why, sure," said Bert, opening the door of the refrigerator and pouring himself a glass of milk. He gulped it down. "But I can only use one hand. You know, I froze the other one, and it's still a little sore."

The cook nodded. "That's all right," he said. "The crate's too heavy for one man, but two can do it."

He swung open the kitchen door, and Bert followed him

out into the passageway that led to the road above. It was a covered passageway, for the snow in late season was so high that it would have been impossible to keep the path to the parking area shoveled. Bert's feet grated on the slippery cleats of the ramp. Ahead he could see sunshine.

As he came out on the level of the parking area, the first thing he saw was a battered jalopy with a ski rack atop. It was Tom Wallace's jalopy, and the old prospector was leaning against the hood. The surly expression on his face deepened to a scowl when he saw Bert. Alan was on the other side of the car, busily loading aboard a pair of jumping skis. Bert could recognize them by their length and by the triple grooves on their soles. He felt an impulse to confront Alan, but as he took a step toward the car, the cook nudged him.

"Okay," said the cook, "here're the bottles." He pointed to a crate full of milk bottles. On either end was a rope. Bert obediently bent over to grasp one end of the case with his left hand, but his angry eyes were turned toward the road. As he stared in that direction, the doors of the jalopy slammed, and the Wallaces were off, their motor coughing and gasping in the rarefied atmosphere. Bert lifted his end of the case and stumbled down the passageway.

From the door of the waxing room, a moment later, he stared out toward the lift and then looked toward the Wallace cabin. There was no smoke coming out of the chimney, and, best of all, there were no skiers between him and the cabin.

If he took a roundabout way through the trees, he certainly could reach the cabin unobserved.

The sun had formed a hard crust under the surface of the snow. After a few hesitating steps Bert knew that the crust would hold his weight. He walked boldly, but always with a wary eye on the crowd of skiers up the hill. They were much too far away to identify him and much too busy with their own skiing. He stopped for a moment and looked at his watch. What its dial told him was reassurance enough. Tom Wallace, in his old car, couldn't possibly be halfway to the jumping tournament.

In the thick forest around the Wallace cabin the shadows were purple. There was a distinct chill in the air. A little breeze stirred the branches and made an uneasy, creaking sound. About fifteen feet from the cabin, Bert stopped and looked around cautiously. He could feel the thumping of his heart.

"Aw, shucks," he said loudly. "There's nobody around." He walked swiftly down the beaten path to the roof of the cabin and reached down with his left hand to pull up the trap door. It lifted easily. As he had suspected, old Tom didn't bother to lock his cabin. Nobody did in the backwoods.

Beneath Bert's feet the rungs of the ladder dropped down into a well of darkness. He put one tentative foot through the trap door and groped with it for the first rung. Then he dropped down into the darkness. It seemed an eternity before his feet finally touched the floor. Instead of the hard boards he had expected, his shoes sank into a soft carpet. He reached into his pocket for a match and scratched it on the sole of his foot. In the faint light he could see that he was walking on a luxurious Persian carpet.

Bert glanced quickly around the rest of the room, taking in as much as he could in the flickering light from the match. The flame burned his fingers and he blew it out.

"Whew," he said to himself. "No wonder he doesn't encourage visitors, living like this." He struck another match. In its glow he was able to distinguish a kerosene lamp on a table in the corner of the entranceway. Before the match had quite gone out, he was able to reach the table and to lift

the glass chimney from the lamp. It was still warm to his hands, indicating that not much time had elapsed since the Wallaces had left their house. The chimney trembled in his hands, and he put it down on the table. He lit another match and applied it to the blackened wick of the lamp. As it flamed up, he put the chimney back in place. Now he had a light, and he could move more freely. He picked up the lamp, cradling it in both hands.

A massive, carved walnut door barred his way. He leaned against it, and it swung open on well-oiled hinges. In the little pool of light shed by the lamp he could see that he was in a large living room. All along one wall were books, racked high on the shelves. Bert felt a sinking feeling in his stomach. How ever would he able to find an old mining register in all that mass of documents?

He walked across the room on another luxurious rug, whose reds and greens glowed dully in the light from his lamp. He set the lamp on a table, reached up to the topmost shelf, and began to pull down dusty books. It was an exasperating task. There seemed to be everything *but* a mining register—old copies of *Godey's Lady's Book,* no doubt an inheritance from an earlier Wallace, sets of Balzac, Dickens, and contemporary novelists of the '90s and early 1900's, books for children, and even a set of the *Encyclopedia Britannica*—but no mining register.

Bert kept doggedly at work, glancing now and then at his watch. There was still plenty of time before the old man could return. He had finished two shelves, and there were still three more to go. Acrid, choking dust swirled up into his lungs as he pulled loose books that apparently had not been read in many years. By now he was beginning to run across volumes that had some direct reference to mining— bound volumes of the U. S. Geological Survey, each of which he studied carefully, looking through the chapter headings to make sure that there were no references to mining at Sunmount. One article on mining in Utah caught his attention, but it turned out to be a highly technical discussion of methods of smelting silver ore, and he laid it down disgustedly. It seemed that the air in the room was growing very heavy, perhaps because the light of the lamp was beginning to exhaust the oxygen. He sank down in an overstuffed sofa to rest for a moment.

The lamp began to give off a strange, yellow light, and Bert swung his head around to glance at it. The wick was smoking and sputtering. Through the glass of the chimney he could see what was happening. A tongue of black smoke was beginning to darken the chimney. Not a bit of kerosene remained. Frantically Bert looked for another lamp. He sprinted out to the anteroom, but none was to be found. He had flung open a little doorway leading into the kitchen when the lamp gave a final sputter and died. He was plunged into blackness.

"I'd better get out of here," he said to himself, feeling a cold chill down his spine. He felt his way toward the ladder. And then, over his head, he heard a shuffling noise, and his heart gave a convulsive leap.

Somebody was coming down! He pressed himself back against the wall and heard the squeak of the trap door as it was flung back. On the floor of the hallway a square of light illuminated the strange, writhing figures of medieval dragons that ornamented the rug. A pair of heavy boots, topped by denim trousers, made their appearance at the top of the ladder.

Bert was trapped.

Lost Man's Basin

High on the pass the spring sun beat down with blinding force on the little party of skiers, and the snow threw back a thousand flashing spears of light. Up at the head of the line Howard Walton pushed his ski cap back on his head and mopped his glistening forehead.

"Whew," he said, " this is getting to be too much for me. I must have too many clothes on." He looked down ruefully at his flannel shirt, which was dampened by perspiration, and stopped on a little knoll, leaning forward on his ski poles for a rest.

Mary Sue, who was just behind him, unshouldered her light pack and rolled up her sleeves. "Better take off your shirt," she suggested. "As long as we're climbing, you certainly won't get chilly."

From the back of the line came a "Hey!" and Howard

looked around at his older brother.

"How much farther, Mary Sue?" he said to the blond girl, who was busy slathering lotion on her arms.

"Oh, quite a few miles," she said, "but pretty soon it'll be downhill and then cross-country for a way. We have to go over the top of this ridge just ahead of us and then drop down through some canyons into Lost Man's Basin."

Ed took a quick squint at the sun, a fiery ball beating down from a point above Hollis Mountain. He stared down thoughtfully at his wrist watch, whose polished steel case reflected the rays of the sun.

"It's nearly noon," he said, "and it looks to me as if we'll have to move right along to hit the cabin. And then what? Can we get back before dark?"

"Oh, sure," Mary Sue said reassuringly. "There's another route back. Goes off to the west, curves around Basin Mountain, and leads us right into the head of the Sunmount Valley. The only thing we have to be careful about is to keep away from the slopes of Basin Mountain and to stay in the middle of the valley floor. There's avalanche country on both sides, I'm sorry to say."

"Okay," Howard broke in. "Then let's go." He swung his pack over his bare shoulders, lifted one ski pole as a signal to the climbers behind him, and began a rhythmic, plodding movement up the hill.

The top of the ridge, where a few gaunt trees stood sentinel, looked close at hand, but the climbers quickly discovered that it was a long distance away. Their course led them uphill in long zigzags; and, from the valley floor far below, the track would have looked like a series of enormous Z's. They did little talking, for talking caused them to get out of breath. Mostly they just plugged ahead, left ski and right pole forward, slide the skis; right ski and left pole forward, slide the skis and push. It was easier, they had discovered, to look down at the snow than to keep on looking ahead at the crest of the ridge, which seemed so near and was yet so far.

At last, however, Ed looked up from his position at the end of the line to see Howard silhouetted on the skyline. An exultant yodel came ringing down.

As the others came up to the top of the ridge, the sight below made them catch their breath. Rolling slopes of snow dropped down toward the narrow V of a canyon, at whose unseen bottom could be heard the rumble of water. Far out across the ridges the canyon opened onto a snowy plain, in the middle of which the glint of ice revealed the outline of a tiny lake. Beyond it, just a dot on the snow, was a cabin.

"That's it!" said Mary Sue jubilantly. "That's Lost Man's Cabin!"

"Looks miles away," sighed Howard. He shielded his eyes as he stared down at the promised land.

"But where is our route home?" asked Ed. "All I see is a network of valleys off to the west. Which one do we take?"

"It's easy to establish," said Mary Sue. "You see that rock outcropping that looks like a face? That's Indian Face Rock, and the canyon we take is just to the left of it."

"But what happens if we make a mistake?" asked Ed, still a little doubtful.

"Well, we can't get very far," said Mary Sue. "The other canyons all lead off into dead ends or else drop down in cliffs. There's only one way out—by way of Indian Face."

"Okay," said Howard, who had been listening closely to this explanation. "And I've got a map and a compass, so we shouldn't have any trouble. Now let's eat."

Again he unslung his pack. He stamped out a fairly hard-packed place for himself in the snow and then unsnapped his ski bindings.

"Watch this," he said to Mary Sue and Betty. "The Walton luxury sofa for skiers. Someday I'm going to patent it and make myself a million dollars."

He jammed his two skis into the snow, tails down and about three feet apart. Then he deftly slid his two ski poles through the steel bindings and sat down on a springy chair with his rucksack at his side. From the pack he extracted a Thermos bottle and two neatly wrapped sandwiches.

"This is the life!" he sighed as he unscrewed the lid of the Thermos bottle, pulled out the cork, and let the steaming hot cocoa pour into the metal cup.

"Pour in a little snow, Howie," said Ed, who had done just that. Howard scooped up a pinch of snow and dropped it into the cup. He put the cup to his lips again, inhaled luxuriously, and swallowed down the steaming contents.

"Have a salt tablet," said Mary Sue, who had made herself a seat from her skis and poles just a foot or so behind him. She handed him a pellet. Howard wrinkled his nose.

"Ugh," he said. "I don't like salt. Why do I need this?"

"Simple, dope," broke in Ed. "You've been perspiring, haven't you?"

"Yeah," said Howard, "but what's that got to do with my taking a salt tablet?"

"Plenty," said Ed. "When you perspire, you lose salt from your body. Take one of these salt tablets, and maybe another one when we get to the cabin, and you'll have replaced most of that salt."

Howard made a face and popped the tablet into his mouth, washing it down with cocoa. "It didn't taste too bad," he admitted grudgingly. "In fact, it didn't taste at all." He stripped the oiled paper from a roast beef sandwich and bit appreciatively into it.

Ed, a few feet away, munched thoughtfully at his own sandwich and stared out at the spectacular view. Finally he swallowed the last morsel, downed the rest of his cocoa in a single gulp, and looked again at his watch.

"We'd better get going, boys and girls," he announced. "Time's-a-wastin'." He pulled his skis from the snow and stripped off the sealskin climbers, which he wound around his waist. "Mary Sue," he said, "you can lead, if you want to. We'll follow you down, since you know the way."

"Okay," said Mary Sue, tucking her ski cap away in her pack. Her blond curls reflected the sunlight as she pulled loose her sealskins and tucked them into her pack. She shouldered the pack, kicked her boots into the ski bindings, swung shut the clamps, and said, "Let's go." She stood poised for a minute on the top of the slope and then dived forward in a long, straight run down across the bumps and hummocks before she made her first turn, a long, controlled, beautiful swing that left a plume of snow trailing its silvery particles in the air behind her. The others followed, almost in her track but not quite, so that they could take advantage of the unbroken snow. Howard, second in line, let out a whoop of joy. Betty and Ed, third and fourth, respectively, skied silently, concentrating on the difficult terrain ahead.

Mary Sue was skiing fast—faster, in fact, than she normally did because the snow conditions were so perfect. The route she took led her down toward the top of the canyon and eventually on to a flat space which reflected the sunlight with a glitter different in appearance from that of the snow higher up.

Her track dropped lower and lower, until at last she plunged over a knoll and down in one last dizzying descent to the flat area visible from above, its snow gleaming dully. She put her skis together for the run-out and leaned far forward to counter her speed and the gradient of the slope. Then, as those behind could see, she suddenly staggered, lurched, spun over her tips and disappeared in a flurry of snow.

"Wet snow!" Howard called back in a warning voice

to Betty and immediately put in several rapid check turns to reduce his speed. He came over the top of the knoll slowly enough to open his tips in a snowplow. This carried him down to the flat at a pace that was barely fast enough to keep him moving. On the flat he lurched a little but stayed upright as he put his skis together and poled over to Mary Sue. She was lying in a heap in the snow, one ski partly under her body. Her face was a chalky white.

"Are you all right?" asked Howard, bending over her in concern.

"I—I don't know," stammered Mary Sue. "My ankle—" She closed her eyes and lay still. Ed and Betty had by now joined the other two skiers.

"That confounded wet snow!" said Ed. "I almost tripped myself. When you run from powder snow into the wet stuff it almost always trips you."

"That's right," said Howard, "and Mary Sue took a bad fall, too." He quickly kicked off his skis and bent over beside Mary Sue, who had opened her eyes once more.

"Let me do it," Ed said sharply. "Give me your first-aid equipment."

Howard pulled loose the knot that held the top of his rucksack together and reached in for the first-aid equipment. Ed, meanwhile, was carefully moving Mary Sue.

"Does that hurt?" he asked. "I mean, does it hurt badly?"

"No," said Mary Sue weakly. "It just throbs a little. I don't believe it's broken."

"Neither do I," said Ed reassuringly. He gently pressed Mary Sue's right ankle, the one that had been twisted beneath her. Then, unsnapping her ski binding, he carefully lifted the foot away from the ski and stretched it out in front of her. Betty, apprehension on her face, unsnapped the other binding, collected the two skis, and stuck them in the snow off to one side.

"It's a sprain all right," Ed said to Howard, who held the first-aid equipment in his two hands. "Now let's put a bandage on it so that Mary Sue can get down to the cabin. Give me that gauze, please." He swiftly unlaced Mary Sue's boot and wound the gauze around her ankle so that it formed a stirrup. Then he slid the boot back on again.

"This will be a tight fit," he remarked, "but if we left the boot off, your ankle would swell up, Mary Sue. This way you'll be able to ski down slowly, and when we get to the cabin we'll put cold and hot compresses on the ankle to reduce the swelling." He laced the boot tightly, and Mary Sue smiled up at him.

"Now try to stand," he said. He offered his ski pole to Mary Sue, who put her full weight on it and slowly rose to her feet, keeping the injured foot a little off the snow. Very carefully she tried her weight on the injured ankle.

"Hurts," she said, "but when I get my ski on and my weight distributed, it won't be so bad."

Howard closed his rucksack and picked up her skis. He set them in the snow beside her and Mary Sue, resting her weight on Ed, slipped her feet into the bindings. Howard bent over and snapped them shut while Ed handed Mary Sue's ski poles to her.

"Okay," Ed said. "Howard, you go first. Mary Sue, you'll be second. I'll follow you, and Betty can follow me. Take it easy on the steep slopes but run straight on the places where there's a flat beyond, if you can see from Howard's skiing that you won't be running into wet snow."

Mary Sue nodded and set her chin at a determined angle. Howard pushed off, skiing in slow, sweeping stem turns, and Mary Sue followed him, wincing a little every time she had to put her weight on her injured ankle. The route dropped down over billowing snow fields, closer and closer to the Basin, until at last Howard swung his right ski pole in the air, put his skis together, and slid down the last slope.

"It can't be far now," said Ed. He glanced at his watch and shook his head.

Mary Sue, who was watching him, said anxiously, "What's the trouble? Getting late?"

"Yeah," said Ed. "It's two thirty now, and we've still got a ways to go. Tell me, is there firewood in the cabin?"

"Yes, and a toboggan, too," said Mary Sue. "The ski patrol takes care of that. The ranger comes around about once a week to check up on things."

"That's good, in case we're stuck," Ed said thoughtfully. "We can always wait the night out in the cabin, though I'd rather not." He dug in his ski poles and began to plod thoughtfully ahead. A thin group of pines crowded a little rise just beyond, and when the party came abreast of them, they found themselves looking across the frozen surface of a lake to Lost Man's Cabin.

"A more welcome sight I never did see," remarked Howard. "It wouldn't be any fun, being stuck out here in the snow all night without a fire."

"And without a chaperon," contributed Betty, who was skiing along beside him.

"Well, I don't think we have to worry about a chaperon," Ed said in a casual drawl. "That's been provided for."

"Quit your kidding," snapped Howard, who was tired and beginning to show it.

"No, I mean it," said Ed, staring quizzically at his brother. "Just look behind you."

High on the pass a black dot was dropping down toward them, trailing a plume of snow behind.

"Wonder who it can be?" Howard asked.

"Bet it's Mr. Holliday," said Mary Sue. "It's about time for his weekly inspection trip."

The black dot continued to drop closer and closer, swung behind a hummock of snow, and finally came out on the flat. Mary Sue sank down into a snowbank with a sigh, and the others followed suit. The sun was making them sleepy, and all of them were dozing when the skier they had sighted finally came up.

"Well, what's this?" a familiar voice said, and the boys and girls looked up to see Muldrow Holliday, his tanned face creased in a grin.

"Oh, just another fool touring party that got caught out," Ed drawled. "We had a little trouble—Mary Sue wrenched her ankle, and we started too late to begin with."

"Then I'll have company at the cabin tonight," Holliday observed. "Let me go on ahead and get a fire started." He

swung out across the plain in a steady, rhythmic cross-country step, and the others could hear the creak of rusty hinges as he swung the cabin door open. Smoke was already pouring from the chimney when they came up to the cabin and unsnapped their skis.

"Welcome to Lost Man's Cabin," came Holliday's voice from the doorway. "But don't say you lost one man already?"

"What do you mean—lost one man?" asked Ed, puzzled.

"Well, where's your brother, Bert?" inquired Holliday, the grin on his face giving way to a serious expression. He extended a muscular finger and scratched his right temple.

"Why, he's back at the Chalet," said Ed. "Or else he's out on the ski hill. Or perhaps he went to the jumping tournament."

"Nope," said Holliday. "He isn't at any of those places. I checked up and he didn't go to the tournament. I looked in the bunkroom, and he wasn't there or anywhere else inside the Chalet. And he wasn't on the ski hill."

Ed looked blankly at Howard. He glanced down at his wrist watch and shook his head despairingly.

"Then he's in trouble—real trouble!" he said soberly. "Do you suppose he went to Wallace's and got caught?"

Howard shook his head, a baffled expression on his face. "Beats me," he said. He wheeled toward Holliday and looked at him appealingly. "Can't one or two of us go back?" he pleaded. "Something awful must have happened."

"I'm sorry," Holliday said regretfully. "You couldn't make the Chalet before dark, and you have to go through some risky country—down canyons and past avalanche slopes. The sun has reached those western peaks now, and the avalanches are beginning to come down. Listen!" He held up his hand. In the distance, off to the west, the boys could hear the ominous muttering of an avalanche.

"In the morning we'll start early, before daybreak," Holliday promised. "And I'm not too worried. That brother of yours has more lives than a cat. Depend on it—whatever trouble he gets himself into, he'll get himself out of."

"I hope so," said Ed, walking into the cabin, where a fire crackled cheerfully. He sank into a chair and stared at the leaping flames. Worry gnawed at his mind, and he paid no attention to the hurry and bustle of his companions as they pulled plates and cups from the shelves and made ready for dinner. All he could think of was Bert, his brother, in what could be serious trouble.

21   *Trapped!*

Like a bird fascinated by a deadly snake, Bert found himself utterly unable to move as the booted legs descended the ladder. The light, shining down from above, outlined Tom Wallace's grim face, his unshorn gray whiskers, and his thin lips. In the midst of panic Bert found himself able to breathe a prayer of thanks that the old man had not looked down. Even though the darkness cloaked him protectively, Bert felt that he might have broken and run if Wallace had looked toward him.

"I've got to do something!" he whispered to himself. "I've got to do something!" And just as Wallace stretched out one boot toward the floor, Bert backed into the kitchen. He had found the power of movement again. On tiptoe, walking backward across a slippery floor, Bert moved out of Wallace's range until his hands came up against an unyielding object. It was a door, his fingers told him, and his pounding heart gave a grateful throb. He felt for the handle and found it, a round, wooden knob. As he stood there, his muscles taut and his skin crawling, he could hear Wallace's heavy breathing. Through a crack in the kitchen door, which he had closed quietly behind him, Bert could see a faint light, and then darkness again. There was a low, muttering sound, as if Tom were talking to himself. Obviously, Bert knew, he was looking for the lamp. In terror Bert remembered that he had not replaced it.

"I left it on the living-room table!" he reminded himself. "He'll know that somebody has been here!"

His fingers gripped the knob, and he pulled it toward him. A door opened, silently. Bert backed inside. The smell of floor wax, acrid and penetrating, came into his nostrils. He pulled the door shut and felt cautiously about. His fingers brushed across a long, round piece of wood, obviously a broom or a mop. They lingered for a moment on a piece of corrugated tin suspended from the wall, and he thought, "That must be a dustpan."

There was no knob on the inside of the door, and Bert grasped the molding at the edge of the door and cautiously pulled it toward him. The door swung shut as silently as it had opened, but somehow it was a little harder to close tightly. Even in his panic Bert realized that something must have jammed; but before he could move to test the door again, there was the heavy tread of boots across the living room, and Tom Wallace's loud voice.

"Who's here? Who's here, I say?"

Bert's heart was pounding so loudly that it almost drowned out the sound of that ominous voice. The heavy footsteps died away for a moment, and Bert thought to himself, "He's looking for another lamp. There's just a chance that I can sneak out and up the ladder while he's searching."

The idea heartened him, but just as he put his shoulder tentatively against the door, there was a gleam of light outside, and he could hear the sound of feet approaching. Wallace was mumbling to himself. He seemed to be pacing around the hallway. The beam of light remained constant, and there was the sound of feet on the ladder leading up to the trap door. Bert held his breath. Was it possible that the man might start searching through the woods? And if so, could he make a break for it? Once more he touched his shoulder to the door, and just then there was the sound of rapidly descending feet on the ladder.

The beam of light grew brighter, and Bert huddled within himself as he heard Tom Wallace's heavy tread on the linoleum floor in the kitchen. There was a tickling in his nostrils from the acrid smell of the floor wax. For one agonized moment he thought he was going to sneeze, but he muffled his nose with his hand, and the threatened sneeze did not materialize. The sound of the footsteps lessened, then grew louder. There was a glare of light as the closet door was suddenly flung open, and Bert blinked in the unaccustomed brightness. Just outside, blocking his way, Tom Wallace stood with the lamp held high in one hand. An ugly grin split his wrinkled face.

"I thought so," he said slowly. "I thought you were in there. You're a pretty smart boy, but you overlooked one little thing. When you closed the door, you closed it on your shoelace. I could see it sticking out of the bottom of the door. Now you and me better have a little talk."

Desperation formed a hard lump in Bert's throat. He lunged forward, and Tom Wallace's hand pulled loose from his arm. The old prospector slipped, lurched, and then sat down with a crash on the kitchen floor. The lamp spun from his hand, and its chimney broke with a high, tinkling sound. Bert dived across the floor and out into the areaway, a bellow of rage following him. He started up the ladder as fast as he could go, and his head was out in the blessed sunlight when he felt the hard grip of a hand on his boots. Wallace had caught him. He struggled futilely, and then slowly began to descend the ladder again. "It's no use," he told himself. "I'm caught and I'll just have to take my medicine."

The old prospector shoved him roughly, and Bert spun into the kitchen. A door slammed behind him, and he heard the click of a latch.

"I'll be back," Wallace's voice came hollowly through the door panels. "Don't go 'way, boy. I still want to talk to you."

It seemed to Bert that hours had gone by, but his watch told him that a scant five minutes had elapsed when the latch clicked again and Wallace appeared in the doorway, this time with a flashlight in his hand.

"Now," he said, "you go first. Into the living room. Sit down on the sofa, and we'll have a little chat. I've got a lot to talk over with you."

Bert sank forlornly into the cushions of the sofa and shielded his eyes as Wallace shone the light on his face.

"You were here lookin' for the old minin' registers, weren't you?" Wallace demanded in a low, vicious tone.

"I'm not going to say anything," Bert answered. "If you know why I'm here, suppose you tell me."

"Well, I do know," Wallace snarled. "I've known what you were after ever since you got on the plane with my boy Alan. You wanted to find your uncle's lost mine."

"And what if I did?" Bert said stoutly. "Is there anything wrong in that?"

"Not for you, there isn't," said Wallace, "but for me, there is. You see, I know where that mine is. Matter of fact, I'm gonna take you to it."

"You mean you're willing to let me know where it is? Even if it becomes my family's property?" Bert was dumfounded, and his voice revealed it.

"Well—yes and no," the old man drawled. "I'll let you know where it is, but it won't become the property of your family. You see, I'm just gonna take you up there and leave you with the gold. Maybe you'll get hungry after a while, but you always can eat that gold. Can't you?" He cackled in a high-pitched voice.

"You wouldn't dare to do a thing like that," Bert said in a trembling voice. "My brothers—"

"Your brothers," the old man said slowly, "are going to think that you went skiing by yourself and got lost in an avalanche. Nobody can prove anything on me, and I'll tell 'em I saw you skiing off into avalanche country." The old man grinned. "Right now," he said, "I'll show you the mining register you've been looking for." From the shelves behind Bert he pulled a massive volume. He shone the light on it so that Bert could see the title.

"*Arabian Nights,*" Bert read slowly. "But I don't see what *Arabian Nights* has to do with the mining register."

The old man cackled. "That's where I fooled you," he said. "Look here." He opened the book. Its pages had been hollowed out, and a smaller book had been fitted in the opening. The golden script on the cover of the smaller book was faded by age, but Bert could still make out the words, "Mining Register," and a date in the '90s.

"Yup, that's it," said the old man proudly. "Couldn't find a better hiding place. I picked that book out of the ruins, and the first thing I noticed was the title to your Uncle John's mine. I knew where it was, you see, because I was scoutin' around in those days. So when your Uncle John didn't come back, I went up and did a little more explorin'.

"You see, your Uncle wasn't patient enough. He quit prospectin' because he hit a vein of inferior gold too difficult to dig out and too expensive to smelt. I just kept pickin' away at the same place, and—guess what!" He paused, as if waiting for Bert to ask a question, but when the question did not come, he went on. "I found a vein of almost pure gold. Ever since, I've been bringin' it down little by little. I'm a man of pretty simple taste, and it's paid my way. And," he banged his fist on the opened book, "it's gonna keep payin' my way."

Bert's eyes roved frantically around the room, as if looking for something that would help him to escape. The old man sat watching him and finally chuckled.

"I won't be too mean," he said. "I'll give you matches and candles. There's plenty of runnin' water up there, too." He reached in his pocket and pulled out a matchbox, which he shook and then opened. He counted the matches inside carefully.

"There's six good matches here and about twenty burnt ones," he finally said. "So if you're careful, you'll have enough matches to keep the candles going." He pulled a massive gold watch from the pocket of his dungarees, snapped open the lid, and shone the beam of the flashlight down on the watch face.

"Be a while till it's dark," he said finally. "I'm goin' away for a little while. You kin have the run of the house, but you won't be able to git away. I'll put a boulder on the trap door, so you might just as well sit here and rest." He rose and strode from the room. Bert could hear the clumping of his feet on the ladder, and then the sound of the trap door swinging shut; finally the thud of a boulder atop it. He knew enough of Tom Wallace to be sure that the old man had locked him in. The darkness of the room settled around him. For a while he sat numbly. Finally he slept.

The sound of feet on the roof woke him from a nightmare dream that somehow was less frightening than reality. There was only darkness outside as the trap door was swung back, and through the doorway he could see Tom Wallace backing down the ladder. There was a click as Wallace snapped on his flashlight and walked into the living room.

"One thing I don't understand, Mr. Wallace, is how you caught me," Bert said to the prospector, who had dropped into a chair opposite him.

"Oh, that was simple," said Wallace. "I figgered you'd be snoopin' around, so I set a little trap. I started off for the jumpin' tournament with my boy, but I only took him down to the head of the canyon. I flagged another car there, and they took him to the tournament. Then I turned around and came back up here, just to see what was goin' on. Now git ready, boy. Follow me up through the ladder."

Bert numbly moved out in the hallway behind the massive back of the prospector and followed him up the ladder.

"Now I'll have to blindfold you and put something over your mouth so's you won't holler," Wallace whispered in his ear. Bert could feel the soft pressure of cloth across his eyes and mouth, and then a round, metallic object was pushed against his back. "I'm takin' no chances," Wallace said softly. "You just walk, and I'll keep you on the right path."

Bert's boots slipped on the crusty snow, and for a long time he seemed to be walking uphill. Then he slid abruptly down a bank and could feel beneath his feet the familiar grittiness of the concrete highway. A pressure on his arm guided him down the road, and he began to count the number of paces. At his twenty-seventh step he was abruptly turned to the right again and began to stumble up another bank through a narrow cleft. On either side of his legs he could feel the snow banks through which the path had been trodden. Again he counted paces as the path climbed upward. He had counted to 127 when Wallace abruptly commanded him to stop.

"Okay, now," said the old man. "I'll take off the blindfold and gag. We're well above the valley."

The cloth was removed from his eyes and mouth. Bert rubbed his lips and looked wildly around him. He was in a grove of trees. Far off he could see the mountains shining dimly. A mist was beginning to rise, and Tom Wallace chuckled as he looked at it.

"I guessed the weather right," he said. "I allus do. Tomorrow it's goin' to snow, and then there'll be avalanches."

Bert nodded dumbly. His bare hands tingled in the cold. The metallic object still pressed into his back, but suddenly it was pulled away.

"All right," said Wallace, "keep followin' the track. And don't try to get away. There're cliffs and canyons up here, and you'll never make it."

Bert jammed one hand in his pocket and felt the regular outline of the matchbox. When the path came into the shadow of the trees, he surreptitiously withdrew the box and slid it open, first making sure that Wallace was a little distance behind. He withdrew the six unused matches and slid them into his watch pocket. Then, as he walked, he carefully dropped burned matches on the snow, one about every two hundred feet. It was a long chance, but even if it snowed, somebody might see one or two of those matches. Now and then he slipped a burned match onto a snow-crusted branch alongside the trail. If it worked— *if*— "but it's *got* to work," he said grimly to himself.

Ahead a wide, steep slope loomed up in the half-light of the high mountains. Bert turned and looked inquiringly at Wallace, who was striding silently perhaps twenty feet behind him. "Go ahead, boy," the prospector growled.

"But how about avalanches?" Bert demanded. "Is it safe?"

"Don't you worry, boy," Tom Wallace replied. "I know these slopes like a book. Nighttimes this one is safe. The sun shines on it all afternoon, and sometimes it avalanches, but after dark it's all right. Freezes harder'n a rock. I'll go ahead and kick steps." He swung out and around Bert, keeping his eye on him, and began to kick footsteps in the crusted snow.

"Don't think these are goin' to lead anybody to you," he said. "In the daytime the sun melts 'em right out again, and I go 'round by another, secret way."

Bert followed gingerly, keeping his eyes turned uphill. He did not want to look down, for the slope seemed to plunge out into space. Probably, he thought, out over the cliffs. The thought of it made him dizzy, and he followed closely behind Tom Wallace. At last the miner disappeared into a thicket of alder. Bert followed him, the branches whipping and scratching at his face. Just ahead of them the alders thinned out, and Bert could see a stout, wooden door perhaps ten feet high.

"This is it!" said Wallace cheerily. "Welcome to your future home, the Lost Mine." There was a click and then a clattering sound as he fumbled with a padlock, and next a high-pitched squeak as the door swung protestingly open. Tom Wallace snapped on his flashlight, and the beam illuminated a damp, dripping opening in the mountainside.

"I said there'd be running water," he chuckled, "and there is." He swung his beam downward, and Bert could see a small rivulet that tinkled across the floor of the tunnel. On the walls there was the dull gleam of gold-bearing rock.

"That's what made me rich, boy," Tom Wallace said. "That's gold. Come in and sit down, and I'll tell you the rest of the story about this mine."

He made a sweeping motion with his flashlight. Bert reluctantly walked through the door of the tunnel and sat down on a boulder. There was a scratching sound as Wallace struck a match and lit a candle. In its dim light Bert could see the tunnel stretching far into the distance.

22   *The Mystery Is Solved*

From his mackinaw pocket Tom Wallace drew a chocolate bar. He broke off a morsel and put it in his mouth, then tossed the rest of the candy to Bert, who caught it deftly.

"Better not eat it all at once," he warned his prisoner. "It's the last meal you'll have in a long time."

"That's nothing unusual," Bert retorted. "I'm beginning to see that you wanted me to have my last meal the night we came up the canyon."

"Oh, the rock fall?" asked Wallace, leaning against the wall of the tunnel and shoving his hands into his pockets.

"Yes, that and the way you tried to run us off the road," Bert said. "And all the other things that have been happening to us since we got up here."

"Well, you're a pretty smart little boy," drawled Wallace. "Maybe it's just as well I *did* bring you up here. You figure things out too closely. Much too closely."

"All but what Willis King has to do with this," said Bert. He was consumed with the desire to know all about Tom Wallace's plots.

"Oh, poor old Willis," chuckled Wallace. "That was easy. I just told him you boys were tryin' to steal his gold. His mine's a washout, you know, but the poor old feller's so crazy that he believed me. I swore him to secrecy, and I sort of hoped that he'd see that you didn't come back to the valley, but he let me down."

"Then all his talk about the skeleton was just imagination?" Bert asked angrily.

"Oh, no," drawled Wallace, looking at Bert from narrowed eyes. "There *is* a skeleton up there. That was another feller who got too curious about how I made my money."

Bert felt an icy chill down his back. Up to this moment he had somehow hoped that Wallace had no serious designs on him; that the whole thing would turn out to be a nightmare; or that somehow, by a stroke of luck, he would manage to get free. At last he realized his peril. He buried his head in his hands; but, though he felt like crying, he defiantly refused to do so. He would deny Wallace that final terrible pleasure.

"At least let me show you around the place," Wallace remarked sarcastically. "Since you're going to live here, you ought to know all about it." He left the candle in its niche on the wall and clicked on his flashlight. "Come with me," he said.

Bert followed obediently. Wallace played his light along the walls. "All gold," he said. "Almost pure gold." The tunnel narrowed, and even Bert had to stoop to keep from bumping his head. They rounded an abrupt curve and came to a tumbled mass of boulders. The water which Bert had noticed at the door of the tunnel trickled out from among these rocks.

"Better not fool around in here," said Wallace gruffly. "There's been a couple of rockfalls in this tunnel, and anyway it doesn't go anywhere." He turned his head and looked back at Bert to impress this message on Bert's mind. Bert nodded an acknowledgment.

"Okay," said Wallace, "let's go back." He hesitated and then added, "Me first." He squeezed past Bert, and the round beam of his flashlight picked out the irregular floor and the craggy ceiling, to which a film of dampness clung. At the door to the cave Wallace flung out a hand.

"That's all, kid," he said brusquely. "I'll be leaving you."

He stepped through the door and slammed it shut. Bert could hear a clanking as an iron bar was lowered into place, and then the loud click of the padlock as it was shut.

His first impulse was to hammer on the door, to scream "Let me out!" and to appeal to Wallace not to leave him. But his second impulse, which seemed to come from some newly discovered reservoir of common sense, was to sit down and think it over.

He chose a chunk of rock beside the door and ran his fingers reflectively alongside. It was a tight fit. Mr. Wallace had seen to that. Anyway, he had no tools with which to break down so massive a door. He felt tired.

"The best thing for me to do is to get some rest," he said stoutly to himself. He felt in his pocket for the matchbox and the unburned matches. Satisfied he had them, he walked over and blew out the candle. The ruddy spark of its smoldering wick was the last thing he saw before his eyes closed and he slept, curled up between a boulder and one of the few dry places on the tunnel wall.

Sometime much later he awakened. He looked quickly at his watch. It registered only eleven o'clock—but was it eleven o'clock at night, or eleven o'clock in the morning? He put the watch up to his ear. There was no sound of ticking. He automatically reached for the stem of the watch and turned it vigorously. At least, even if the watch was wrong, it would keep him company. He sat back and took a deep breath.

"Why, that's funny," he said aloud. His voice echoed hollowly in the tunnel. "The air is still fresh. And if the air is still fresh, it must be coming in from somewhere!" He felt his way across the tunnel to the candle, scratched a match, and lit it. Then, on hands and knees, he crawled over to the door and sniffed deeply. He could not be sure that air was coming in, but then a thought occurred to him.

"Why, sure," he said. "I'll test it with the candle." He gently broke the candle from the accumulation of wax that held it in place, and carried it over to the door. Its flame flickered imperceptibly, and then began to lean steadily toward the door. The fresh air in the tunnel was going *out* through the door. It wasn't coming *in* through the door. So it must be coming from the back of the tunnel, and—

Excitedly Bert grabbed the candle and moved to the back of the tunnel. Here the candle flame again bent outward, and his suspicions were confirmed. The fresh air was coming through the rock pile! That meant there must be another opening to the tunnel, despite what Wallace had said! He shielded the candle flame with his hand and sat down on the rock pile to think it over.

What could he use for tools? He couldn't move those boulders with his bare hands, could he? He gently set the candle in another niche hewn out of the side of the tunnel and rested his chin on his hand as he thought out the problem. He furrowed his brow in concentration for a moment, then sprang to his feet, shouting, "I've got it!" He followed this with an "Ouch!" He had forgotten that the top of the tunnel was so low and he had bumped his head.

Nursing it with one hand, he snatched up the candle with the other and made a careful inspection of the tunnel walls. Obviously, if Mr. Wallace mined gold up here, he didn't carry his tools with him each time. They must be hidden somewhere around the tunnel.

But where? He looked at every inch of the walls before admitting in disappointment that he couldn't find the tools. They were nowhere in sight.

"Beats me," he said dejectedly to himself. "Beats me." He sat down hard on the boulder nearest the door. As he did, it tipped suddenly and sent him sprawling to the floor. The candle slipped from his hands and guttered out in a pool of wax. Bert groped for it, struck his second precious match and set the candle back in the niche.

"Doggone rock!" he said and kicked it. The rock hesitated a little, then rolled to one side and clattered to rest. Underneath it was a deep hole hewn from the rock, and in the hole Bert could see, when he lifted his candle higher, a rusty crowbar. He had the tool with which to save himself.

The crowbar was a heavy instrument, and he panted a little as he pulled it up into the light to inspect it. As he had hoped, it was in perfect shape. A wooden-handled pick, which also stood head-down in the hole, he left untouched.

"This is it!" Bert said jubilantly and shouldered the heavy crowbar. Its weight made him stagger a little. He draped his right arm over the bar and grabbed up the candle in his left hand as he moved back to the other end of the tunnel. It was going to be a tight fit, he could see. He mentally measured the distance between walls and looked appraisingly at the boulders. Leaning the crowbar against one wall, he clambered up on the rock pile. There was a question in his mind, but he quickly answered it. He was searching for the key rock, and he had found it—a jagged boulder that seemed to support a whole pile of rocks above. Near the ceiling there was even a little opening. He took a quick look behind him. He had to find a place where he could take refuge if a whole cascade of boulders came down.

"And I've got it!" he announced to himself. On the right side of the tunnel, as he faced toward the rocks, was a projection. He flattened himself in this projection and found that he could pull his whole body out of harm's way—if he moved fast enough. That was all the assurance he needed. Carefully, very carefully, he fitted the crowbar under the key rock. There was just barely space for its slanting point. He leaned on the bar, watching the boulder pile intently. It was beginning to move. Just one more shove downward would do it—and he sprang back into safety as the entire pile came down with a roar that reverberated through the tunnel and sent a hollow echo back to him in his cranny. The last rock settled to rest with a scraping sound, and he peered out cautiously, holding the candle above his head. He gave a whoop of triumph. At the top of the pile gaped a hole big enough for a man to crawl through!

Bert dropped the crowbar, which gave off a dull clang as it landed on the floor of the tunnel, and cautiously wormed his way up through the tumbled rocks. One big boulder, twice the size of his head, was shaky, and he found a way around it.

He snuffed out the candle as he crawled down the other side of the rock pile and felt his way onto the damp floor again before he lit it. The tunnel was lower here, and he almost had to lie on his stomach, pushing the candle ahead of him. He was having to shield the candle flame, for the wind was increasing, and somewhere in the distance he could hear a dull roar as air was sucked in through the tunnel entrance. Then his hands dipped into water, and he lowered his head to look at a glittering pool. It seemed to stretch on ahead for perhaps fifty feet, and it filled the tunnel from wall to wall. At the far end of the pool a barrier of rock seemed to extend down almost to the water, and Bert shivered involuntarily as he appraised his chances. He couldn't go back, to starve. He *had* to go ahead, regardless of what was there.

He carefully extracted the unburned matches from his watch pocket and gave each of them a coating of candle wax. Then he pulled the matchbox from his pocket, put the matches in it, and sealed the box with wax. Finally he let a blob of candle drippings fall on the tunnel floor and snuffed out the candle wick in this. Reassured that he would have matches and a candle if he ever reached a dry place again, he crawled forward into the icy water.

At first it was shallow, and his shirt buttons caught on the irregular stones as he moved ahead. Suddenly the pool deepened, and he found himself swimming, the candle clutched in one hand. His head bumped rock, and he realized that he had come to the barrier.

"Nothing ventured, nothing gained," he said stoutly and ducked his head as he plunged under water. The rock of the barrier scraped and caught at his shirt but he lunged through. In a moment he was past the barrier and crawling damply out of the water and onto a blessedly dry shelf of rock. To his right he could hear the gurgling of the stream as it poured out of a hole in the wall. Ahead the wind was still moaning, and it was far colder than it had been on the other side of the rock barrier.

"Now we'll see if the candle will work," he remarked to himself. He peeled the layer of wax from the matchbox, then from the match itself, and finally from the candle wick. He held his breath as he struck the match, but it flamed brightly, and so did the candle, though the wind threatened to blow it out. The wind, in fact, was increasing in intensity. Against his face, Bert suddenly felt the sting of something wet. He looked down at his soaking sleeve. A snowflake glistened there before it vanished into moisture.

He thought he had never seen anything so beautiful as that flake of snow, that evidence that a world outside still existed.

The tunnel veered sharply to the left, and ahead of him Bert could see a dull blur. It took him a minute to realize what it was. Then he blew out the candle and said softly to himself, "Snow—daylight—freedom!" He hurried forward, able to stand upright as the tunnel ceiling rose, and plunged past a broken, splintered wooden door into daylight. There was a blizzard blowing, and though he shielded his eyes, Bert could see scarcely five feet ahead. He felt his way gingerly forward, but came to an abrupt stop at the edge of a cliff. Very carefully he made the circuit of what seemed to be a little platform. The storm and snow lifted for a moment and, with a pang of disappointment, he could see the remains of an old road winding across the cliffs—but with a ten-foot gap separating him from it. A section of the roadway, at some time in the past, had slid away, and he was trapped.

"Trapped, but not licked," Bert said to himself, and shook his fist defiantly at the snowy skies. "I've got matches. I've got wood, and I've still got most of a candy bar. Someday this storm will let up, and then they'll see me."

23   *Race Against Time*

Inside the cabin in Lost Man's Basin, Howard Walton tossed restlessly under the weight of his blankets. It was hot in the cabin. Holliday had stoked the little stove in the middle of the room until it literally bulged with firewood. Now, at six in the morning, the last of the wood was burning itself out. There was a thump, and a rustling sound, as a log rolled down against the side of the stove. Howard yawned drowsily, pushed back his blankets, and turned on his right side to go back to sleep. His nose almost brushed the windowpane, and on its tip he felt a familiar, prickling coldness. Snow!

It was Holliday who rose first. The ranger slipped heavy socks on his feet and tiptoed over to the stove. He lifted the lid as carefully as he could and stared down inside. The last of the fire was dying away; a few embers still glowed in a conical pile of ashes. He carefully reached for some kindling wood and dropped it onto the embers, then took a deep breath and blew into the opening on top of the stove. In a moment he was rewarded by a faint, crackling sound as the tiny slivers of kindling burst into flame. He dropped in some larger wood and reached for the ax he had carried in his pack. As he touched the ax, which had been resting against the side of his bunk, it wavered and then tipped over. The clattering sound woke everyone.

"Look at the snow!" Howard said, gesturing toward the window. "Don't tell me we're going to be stuck here another day!"

"Of course not," the ranger reassured him. "It may be a little tougher going, but we'll get out."

Holliday pulled a small frying pan from his rucksack, and then a brown paper package. Soon bacon was frying. The aroma filled the air, and both boys hurried to slip into their boots.

"Sure smells good," said Howard, rubbing his hands together. He started toward the stove to look into the frying pan and almost collided with Betty.

"I'm afraid we're having some trouble," she said seriously. "Mary Sue's ankle has swollen so much she can't get her boot on. Maybe you'd better look at it, Mr. Holliday. She's dressed now, all but the one boot."

Holliday swept back the canvas curtain and dropped to his knees beside Mary Sue, who was sitting on the bunk with her injured leg drawn up in the air. Even with its swathing of two thick socks, it was evident that her ankle had swollen. Holliday pressed it gently, and Mary Sue tried unsuccessfully to fight back a moan of pain.

"I'd better take off the socks and see what's underneath," Holliday said. He rolled down the layers of wool, and shook his head when the ankle came into view. It had puffed out to twice its normal size. The skin was red and shiny.

"Looks bad," he said. Ed, who had knelt beside him, assented.

"Well, fortunately there's a first-aid toboggan here," said Holliday. "We can put Mary Sue on and take turns dragging the toboggan."

"But—what about Bert?" broke in Howard excitedly. "Couldn't I go on ahead and get a searching party started? You can't tell what might have happened to him by now."

Holliday rose to his feet, turned, and put a hand on Howard's quivering shoulder. It was a firm hand, and its pressure somehow reassured Howard.

"I'm sorry, kid," the ranger said. "But there are two reasons why we'll all have to go in together. First of all, this is avalanche country, and it would take a skier who was thoroughly familiar with the terrain to get down through the canyons to the valley and the Chalet. Second, we have to take care of Mary Sue. It will take two of us to change off on the toboggan when we're going across level land, and it will take all three of us men to get it through the canyons."

Howard swallowed and then nodded grudgingly. "I can see your point," he said, "but I'm worried about Bert."

"And so are we all," said Holliday. "But I'm inclined to believe that he's all right, knowing Bert, and a few hours more are not likely to make any difference. After all, isn't it better to have all of us get back safe and sound than it would be to send you on ahead and have you lost in an avalanche?"

"Well—yes," admitted Howard. "I'll just forget about my worries for a while. Now who's ready for breakfast? I know *I* am."

"And so are we," called out Mary Sue from her bunk. She smiled at Howard, and that somehow cheered him. Holliday, meanwhile, took the bacon from the frying pan and set it to drain on the sheet of brown paper in which it had been wrapped. Into the grease that sputtered in the pan, he cracked four eggs and carefully watched them as they fried to a golden color. Then he deftly slid each egg onto a slice of bread, also extracted from his magic pack, and handed them out to the boys and girls.

"You eat the eggs," he said. "I'll dine on bacon. I had a good luncheon at the Chalet before I came over the pass yesterday."

It was not a big breakfast, but it was a satisfying one and quickly eaten. Howard surreptitiously licked his fingers as he finished his piece of bread-and-egg and then set to work making up his bunk. Ed, whistling tunelessly as he always did when worried, imitated his younger brother. Mary Sue, hopping on one leg, tried to do her share, but finally gave up and let Betty do the bed-making.

"Okay, boys," Holliday finally said, "let's get the toboggan. It's just around the corner of the house."

The snow beat wetly down on their faces as the ranger and two boys felt their way around the end of the cabin. The toboggan, which stood on end, was easily lifted down, and they brought it back to the front door, trailing a length of cord behind.

"Okay, Mary Sue," Holliday called out cheerfully. "Have Betty help you over here, and we'll tie you on to the toboggan." In a moment Mary Sue hopped out through the door, her wind jacket buttoned tightly and her ski cap pulled down over her ears. She stretched out on the toboggan, and Holliday expertly lashed her in place.

"Stick close to me," Holliday warned as Betty and the boys huddled around him. He consulted a compass which he held steady in the palm of his hand, took a bearing that satisfied him, and then pointed off into the storm. "That's our direction." He picked up the toboggan rope and looped it over one arm as he kicked his boots into his bindings. He snapped the cable shut and transferred the toboggan rope to his shoulders.

"Okay," he said. "Let's go." He took off at a steady pace. Betty dropped into place behind the toboggan, and the two boys skied along, one on either side. For what seemed an eternity they moved along through a yellowish haze, neither climbing nor going downhill. Finally a rock promontory loomed up on their right.

"That's Indian Face," said Holliday, relief in his voice. "We're on the right track. But now we start going down through the canyons." He turned to Ed. "Take the rope at the back of the toboggan and hold the toboggan back as we go downhill," he directed. "I'll snowplow and go slow, and I'll let you know when I'm going to turn. Be careful now!"

"You bet," Ed said. Howard dropped into line behind him, with Betty at the end of the little procession.

"Let's go," Holliday called out and put his skis together.

Soon all of them were whistling down through the blizzard, flying faster and faster, until finally their skis began to ride out on the flat place Holliday had predicted. As they stopped to catch their breaths, there was a rumbling sound from somewhere high above and behind them. The rumble grew into a roar that echoed back and forth across the canyon and was mimicked by a distant noise on some far-away peak.

"That's what I meant," said Holliday quietly. "The snow cornice just came down."

He passed a hand across his forehead, as if brushing away an unpleasant thought, and then took up his position at the head of the toboggan. Without saying a word, Howard took the rear rope from Ed and opened his skis into snow-plow position. Again they wound their way down through the canyon. At one point they passed close to a rushing stream and stopped for a drink. Mary Sue had dropped off to sleep on the toboggan, her ski cap pulled well down over her eyes.

"We're almost out in the main valley," Holliday said reassuringly. "Then we'll have a long cross-country pull into camp." He took up his position again at the head of the toboggan and plodded out across the flat. Now and then clusters of trees began to show up dimly through the wall of falling snow. Howard looked twice at his watch as the long trip continued. The first time he looked, the watch hands registered two o'clock; the next time, three o'clock. At the head of the line Holliday suddenly let loose with an exultant yodel.

"There's the Chalet!" he yelled back, gesturing toward a darker spot in the mist. A few feet more and the building was plainly visible, its lights glowing against the curtain of falling snow. Howard went forward and grabbed one end of the looped toboggan rope and strained his weight against it. Ed sidestepped ahead, up the last little knoll, and then flung open the door of the waxing room.

A flood of light poured out as Howard and Holliday, their skis still on their feet, scraped across the concrete floor with the toboggan and Mary Sue behind them. Two startled skiers, busy with a waxing job, looked down at the toboggan and then sprinted for the staircase. Ed and Howard, kicking off their skis, followed them.

Behind the desk a drowsy clerk looked up at them in surprise as they asked for Bert.

"But I thought he was with you!" he protested. "We haven't seen him since yesterday afternoon!"

From behind them came the clumping of feet as Holliday and two other men, strangers to the boys, carried Mary Sue through the living room and upstairs to her bed.

"I'll bet I know who can tell us what's happened to Bert!" Howard cried suddenly. "Mr. Wallace—if he's home. Let's go down and see him."

"Take it easy," said Ed slowly. "I believe now that he does know where Bert is, but let's not take chances. We'll ask Mr. Holliday to go with us when we talk to him."

As he spoke, Holliday walked down the stairs and out to the desk. Ed quickly explained what he had in mind, and Holliday nodded his agreement.

"This calls for a careful investigation," he said. "Come with me, and we'll go see old Tom." He led the way to the door, walked down the steps, and then wallowed out through the snow toward the Wallace cabin. There was the acrid smell of wood smoke in the air.

"He's home all right," Howard said grimly. "That smoke comes from his fireplace."

As Holliday and the two boys walked up onto the roof of the Wallace cabin, a voice from below called, "Who's there?"

"Just me and a couple of visitors," Holliday called back. "We want to come in, Tom."

The trap door was flung open, and Tom Wallace stuck his head out. He paled beneath his whiskers as he looked at Ed and Howard, and then said in a surly voice, "I got nothin' to talk to you about." There was a thud as he slammed shut the trap door. Holliday reached down and yanked it open again.

"Come on, boys," he said to Howard and Ed. "We're going down inside." He lowered himself down through the trap door, and the two boys followed him. Below they walked through an anteroom and into the living room, where Wallace sat slouched in a chair staring grimly at them.

"Tom, we didn't come for social purposes," the ranger began without any polite preamble. "Young Bert Walton is missing, and we have a notion you know where he is."

"Me?" demanded the prospector gruffly. "Why should I know anything about the kid?"

"I think you know a lot more about the Walton boys and what they're doing out here than you've told us," Holliday said sternly. "I just want to warn you that the penalty for kidnaping in this state is a severe one."

"And I say I don't know where the kid is and I don't care!" shouted Wallace, pounding the arm of his easy chair for emphasis. His beady eyes glittered and shifted from Holliday to Ed to Howard as he talked.

"Well, for lack of any better proof, we've got to accept that statement," said Holliday. "But since you deny knowing what's become of Bert, perhaps it's possible that in your travels yesterday or today, you ran across some ski tracks going off into the area of one of the old mines—where people don't ordinarily go, you know." The ranger's voice, formerly stern, was now persuasive.

"Since you're talkin' polite to me, I *did* see some of them tracks," said Wallace. His lips parted in what might pass for a grin, and he leaned forward with just a trace of eagerness.

"Where? Where?" demanded Howard, impatient to know. He took a step closer to Wallace.

"Up toward the mountain to the east of Catamount,"

said Wallace. "I was up there lookin' around for another old mine when I saw these tracks leadin' up into the hills. I bet if you search there, you'll find the boy, probably holed up in one of those old diggin's until the storm has passed."

Holliday shook his head gravely. He turned and looked sympathetically at the two Walton boys before speaking.

"That's another bad avalanche area," he said, "and we can't risk a searching party in there during a storm. Boys, I'm afraid we're out of luck until the storm is over."

"And that'll be forty-eight hours from now," contributed Tom Wallace. "I know weather up here, and this is likely to be a long storm." He shook his head, but his lips quivered, almost as if he wanted to smile but didn't dare to do so.

"Licked!" said Howard bitterly. "We're licked." Again he felt a hand on his shoulder and looked up into Holliday's face.

"Don't worry, boy," the ranger said softly. "My bet is that this storm will start clearing sooner than Tom predicts, and then we'll find your brother. Take my word, he'll be all right."

Howard nodded numbly and turned toward the trap door. He felt the pressure of another hand on his shoulder. It was Ed, smiling down reassuringly at him.

24   *The End of the Search*

Back in the cave Bert stirred restlessly and shifted on his bed of stone. A particularly sharp piece of rock was jabbing him in the ribs, and he moaned a little as he tried to escape it. Somehow the rock seemed to follow him wherever he went, and he finally resigned himself to a few more moments of cramped, aching sleep. Finally a gust of wind blew smoke across his face, and he woke, coughing and gagging. With the wind came a splatter of snow.

"Good night!" he said as he struggled upright. "This is getting serious." His knees ached, his chest ached, and his whole body throbbed. He stared out past the entrance to the tunnel and into an inferno of whirling snow. Automatically he consulted his watch. Then he realized, with a wry laugh, that he had no idea whether or not it was right.

"All I really know," he said to himself in a low voice,

"is that I have been here two nights and that I'm getting awfully hungry. Also, I'm running out of firewood." He looked over at the remains of the door. The fire was smoldering, but still burning a little. Not much wood remained.

Hungry. The thought stuck in his mind. He put his hands in his pockets, as if he hadn't already turned them inside out half a dozen times in search of food. Again he pulled out the pockets. Into his hands dropped a tube of ski wax, a couple of coins, and the few matches he had not burned in keeping the fire going. For want of anything better to do, he reached for his parka draped on a boulder and patted its pockets. He hadn't bothered to look in there, for he never kept food in his parka.

"But maybe I'd better look," he cautioned himself. He jammed a hand into one pocket. It came in contact with sticky ski wax smeared inside the pocket, and also touched a long, flat and narrow object. He wondered idly what it could be, and then he suddenly knew. It was a stick of gum! Greedily he pulled it loose from the sticky wax and reverently held it in his palm.

Very carefully and still reverently, he pulled aside the outer wrapping and folded back the tinfoil. The gum was brittle. As he tried to break the stick into two parts, several little fragments fell to the floor of the cave. Bert searched eagerly for them and popped them into his mouth, along with the unbroken half piece. The rest of the gum he stuffed back into the parka pocket.

"This is my breakfast," he remarked to himself. "The other half of the stick will be my dinner. After that—" He thought briefly of the consequences, and a little shudder ran through his body. It was not a nice prospect. He sat down on the boulder and stared out into the snow again.

Was it imagination, or was the storm breaking? Great clouds of snow swirled past the cave as Bert stood in the doorway.

Bert walked out onto the platform and looked carefully around him. In the lessening storm, which still deposited a mantle of white on his shoulders, he could see more clearly the problem that confronted him. To the left of the platform, as he faced out, a giant boulder teetered at the edge of a sheer cliff that dropped down to snowfields below. To his right other boulders stuck their jagged heads out of a snow slope that looked as if it might break loose any minute and go roaring down to the valley as an avalanche. Above his head and over the cave the rock rose sheer.

The snow swirled past in a final suffocating gust of wind, and then the miracle began to take place. Far across the valley peak after peak emerged slowly from a gauzy curtain of snow. Clouds eddied and swirled in the valley below and then withdrew as if whisked away by an unseen hand. In the clear but blinding light, with the sun beating hotly down, Bert could see for miles. That black dot off to his left was the Chalet, with the snowy road winding past it. The lift line was a straight line on the unblemished snow almost directly ahead of him. And off to his right, high up on the mountainside, three figures toiled along, tiny as ants.

Three figures! Why, that must be Ed, and Howard, and Muldrow Holliday, looking for him! Before he realized the futility of what he was doing, Bert let out a feeble yell. The sound was lost in the vastness of the canyon, and the three ant-figures kept climbing upward. Bert looked frantically around him. He dragged the wreckage of the door over to the fire and threw it on top of the flames. A cloud of smoke and a tongue of flame shot up into the clear air. The three figures kept on climbing. By now they were high up on the other mountainside, miles away but probably at almost the same altitude as Bert.

"They've got to see me!" he said grimly. "They've *got*

to!" With a convulsive motion he ran across the platform to the balanced rock and pushed against it with both hands. The rock trembled on its underpinning, tipped forward, and then settled back again. Bert leaned his shoulder against it and could feel the vibration as the mammoth boulder moved an inch or two. Desperate, he sat down in the snow. Behind him was the mountain wall. He rested his back against the stone and shoved with both feet, gritting his teeth. The rock moved slowly, imperceptibly. Bert could feel the strain in his leg muscles, which burned like fire. But the rock was still moving—and at last it broke free, plunged into space, and struck the cliffs below with a roar that must have been audible for miles around.

As the sound was echoing through the canyon, Bert moved forward to the edge of the platform and shaded his eyes against the sun. The climbers across from him had stopped for a moment. They were far too distant for Bert to be able to tell whether they saw him or not, but a few seconds later his heart leaped with delight. One after another the three figures had turned and were swinging down the mountainside, leaving a plume of snow behind them. He watched for ten minutes, until they were out of sight behind the trees. Then he sat down in the warm sun and let its fierce heat bake the stiffness out of his bones. For a little while he dozed.

The clatter of boulders somewhere close at hand woke him from his slumbers. For a few minutes he could not locate the sound, but then he looked far down the mountain slopes. A lone figure was toiling up toward the cave, and, even though it was more than a mile away, Bert felt a chill. It could be no one but Tom Wallace!

"There's nothing to do now but to sit quiet," he reassured himself. "They'll be along in a little while. Maybe they'll even catch up with Wallace before he gets here."

Old Wallace was coming closer, and now his face was visible as a white blur, turned up toward the clump of aspen at the other entrance to the cave. Bert's gaze slid past the prospector and down toward the valley. At last he could see his rescuers, plodding steadily upward. But, even as he watched them, they veered in their path and swung off in the other direction. He was leaning over the edge of the platform, watching them, when there was a shrill whine and a splatting sound. Tiny fragments of rock showered down on him from the jagged wall above, and he ducked involuntarily. He looked down again, and then cowered behind a boulder. Old man Wallace was scarcely three hundred yards away, and he was firing at him! Another bullet ricocheted off the rock, and he heard a hoarse, bellowing sound.

"I've got to turn those people around!" Bert said frantically, thinking of the rescue party, growing smaller in the distance. He dropped to his stomach and crawled to the opposite side of the platform. He reached out one hand and touched the nearest boulder that jutted above the snow. It trembled beneath his fingers. He jammed his arm in the space behind it and gave a wrench that sent a spurt of pain up through his arm. The boulder quivered, moved, and then began to roll. Before Bert's eyes the blanket of snow peeled away in the wake of the moving boulder and began to slide majestically downhill. There was only the sound of the boulder at first. Then there was a roar louder than Bert had ever before heard, and a great cloud of snow shot up from the slopes somewhere below. Before this cloud thickened and hid the valley from sight, Bert could see great trees being snapped by the force of the avalanche like matchsticks. He held his breath at the immensity of the slide he had started. As the snow cloud gradually subsided, he looked cautiously across at the slope up which Tom Wallace was climbing.

The prospector stood there, staring upward, as if paralyzed by fear. Suddenly there was another blood-curdling roar, and the entire snow slope slid apart fifty feet above him. Wallace turned and frantically began to run, but he was too late. The new avalanche swept him down, over a rise of ground, and out of sight. Then, much later, the lethal snow cloud rose skyward. Bert let out a tremulous sigh and sank down on a boulder. His heart was pounding, and he felt dizzy and breathless. From far off he heard the sound of a shot. The rescue party must have seen him! He rose to his feet, picked up his parka and waved it frantically.

Steadily the three figures came closer and closer until he could distinguish faces. His suspicions were correct. Holliday, Ed and Howard had come to rescue him! They reached the edge of the first avalanche area and paused a minute. Bert cupped his hands for a megaphone and shouted out to them, "Be careful! Avalanches!"

A shout and an acknowledging wave came back to him, and the three figures began to move out across the slope that had carried Tom Wallace away. Soon Bert could see the broad grin on Ed's tanned face. He leaned out over the edge of the platform and extended his hand to Holliday, who was in the lead. The ranger accepted it, then vaulted lightly to the platform. Howard and Ed followed.

"Boy, I'm the luckiest fellow in the world!" Bert finally said and sat down again on a rock. Holliday shrugged his pack from his shoulders and undid the drawstring.

"Want a sandwich?" he asked, handing two of them to Bert.

"Do I?" said Bert hungrily and began to wolf down the food. From Holliday's pack there came a Thermos bottle and a cup which the ranger filled with steaming cocoa. Between mouthfuls of food and cocoa Bert stared happily at his two brothers.

"I thought you'd never find me," he finally said with a contented sigh, leaning back against the rock wall. "And then I thought you'd get caught in an avalanche, just as Wallace did."

"Yeah, we saw him go," said Holliday. "But those avalanches cleaned off all the snow, so it was perfectly safe for us to cross."

"I didn't intend to have him come to such a terrible end," Bert said thoughtfully. "I set off *my* avalanche over here at the end of the platform. I figured it might frighten him away. The next thing I knew, the other avalanche had started, too."

"That often happens," said Holliday, sipping his cup of cocoa. "When one avalanche is let loose, it weakens the structure of the snow, and a second one very often follows. You might say that Tom Wallace asked for it; he should have known better than to get out on such dangerous slopes just after a storm."

"Well, I guess he figured he had to come up here to make sure that we didn't find Bert," Howard broke in. "When the sun came out and his weather forecast proved wrong, he probably got panicky. If that was the case, he probably forgot all about danger, about everything but Bert."

"I guess that's right," Holliday agreed. "And now tell me —what is this cave? Just another abandoned working?"

"Nope," said Bert proudly. "Come with me." He led the way into the musty interior of the cave and struck one of his last matches. In its light the dull gleam of gold particles could be seen on the cavern walls. Holliday pulled a flashlight from his pocket and inspected the flakes carefully. Finally he turned and stuck out his hand.

"Congratulations," he said, shaking Bert's hand. "If this is your uncle's cave, you're rich. This time it's real gold —not fool's gold."

"Well, it's Uncle John's cave all right," Bert said proudly. "Wallace told me so."

"First you'd better tell us how you got up here," Ed interrupted. "Sounds to me as if you took one chance too many."

"Yup, I almost did," Bert confessed. "You see, when you went touring, I decided to sneak over to Wallace's cabin to look for the mining register that carried the deed to Uncle John's mine. While I was looking through the library, Wallace caught me.

"He told me he was bringing me up here to starve, said he was going to pretend that he didn't know what happened to me. He figured that by the time you found out where I was, it would be too late. First, however, he showed me the mining register, and then he brought me up here. He locked me in, but I managed to find a way through a rock fall and out onto this platform.

"And now," he said, "there's one Wallace still to be reckoned with. I mean Alan. Let's go down and pay a call on him at his home."

With Holliday out in front the little party moved cautiously down over the avalanche slopes. The mountainside dropped away steeply in front of them, but at last they came to the fan of the avalanche. Bert looked in amazement at the tangle of trees, boulders, and huge chunks of snow he had set loose.

Below the avalanche fan Holliday broke trail through the feathery snow. Bert followed last in line, grateful to be spared this tiring work. The snow was waist deep, and he was more weary than he cared to admit. On a sunny promontory, where the snow had melted or blown away, the party halted.

"Seems good to see buildings and highways, and—and cars moving around," Bert said, pointing to an auto that moved out of the parking space.

"Yeah," said Holliday, looking intently toward the valley. "And if I'm not mistaken, that's Tom Wallace's old jalopy. Maybe we'd better get on down and see what's happening."

Bert rose to his feet and dropped into line behind Holliday. The glitter of the sun on the snow hurt his eyes, and he could not see the moving car very clearly. It was a long way below them, and they still had a long climb down. He settled down to a steady walking pace, slipping a little in the loose, floury snow. Finally Holliday stepped up over a pile of snow and disappeared from sight. Bert climbed over the same ridge, and then his feet went out from under him. Sliding and tumbling, he finally came to a halt at the edge of the road.

"Home again!" Bert said with a sigh. Across the road from them cars were parked, and beyond was the familiar brown clapboarding of the Chalet. He got slowly to his feet and followed Holliday across the road, down the ramp he had never expected to see again, and into the living room. The drowsy clerk raised his eyebrows in surprise as Bert walked through the door.

"Why—why I thought you must have been caught in an avalanche!" he stammered.

"Nope," said Bert, "I wasn't, but Tom Wallace was. Now all I want to know is, where is Alan Wallace?"

"Why, he's gone," said the clerk. "He came running in here white as a sheet a while ago, and phoned down to the city for a plane reservation. And then he came by the door with his bags a little later. The cook told me he jumped into his dad's car and took off down the canyon."

"Did you hear him say where he was going?" Bert asked sharply.

"Come to think of it, I did," said the clerk, scratching his head. "Boston, as I remember it."

"Boston!" said Bert to his brothers. "That's right close to home. Come on—let's go down to the cabin and see if he got away with the mining register."

After floundering through the snow, the three boys clattered up on the roof of the Wallace cabin, flung open the trap door, and hastily lowered themselves inside. Below, a lamp burned dimly on the hallway table. In his hurry Alan had not even bothered to put it out. Bert snatched up the lamp and led the way into the living room.

"Here, hold it," he said, thrusting the lamp at Ed. He stood on the sofa and looked quickly down the rows of dusty books. Finally his hand shot out and he yanked down the volume for which he was searching. He flipped it open and gave a deep sigh. The mining register was still there.

"Take a look," he said, handing the book to Howard. His younger brother pulled the register from its hiding place and flipped the pages quickly.

"Good grief, here it is!" Howard burst out and handed the book to Ed. The older brother glanced down the yellowed page.

"Allow me to shake your hand," he said to Bert. "This settles it. We're rich."

"Oh, boy!" Howard yelled. "New skis, new boots, and maybe another trip this summer!"

"Well, yeah," Bert said. "After all, we share and share alike in this. Tomorrow we'll call on Mr. Wilson and let him register the deed in our names."

"What'll you do with *your* share of the money, Bert?" asked Ed, who had dropped into a chair with the register still in his hand.

"One thing I'm surely going to do is to buy one of those metal canoes," said Bert.

"And go on a canoe trip up in Maine?" Howard burst out. "Hot dog!"

"Yeah, we might," said Bert. "We'll let Dad handle the money from the mine, and we'll go take a long vacation somewhere up in the north woods."

"A long way away from avalanche country," said Howard. "And a long way away from the Wallaces."

"Well, don't forget that Alan is going to be somewhere in the East," Bert said reflectively. "But we can handle him. When we Walton boys stick together, we can do anything."

Famous Classics

Meet wonderful friends—in the books
that are favorites—year after year

Fiction for Young People

ROY ROGERS
The Enchanted Canyon

DALE EVANS
Danger in Crooked Canyon

ROY ROGERS AND DALE EVANS
River of Peril

DRAGNET

TARZAN
The Lost Safari

GENE AUTRY
The Ghost Riders
Arapaho War Drums

**TROY NESBIT'S
MYSTERY ADVENTURES**
The Diamond Cave Mystery
Mystery at Rustlers' Fort

GINNY GORDON
The Lending Library
The Broadcast Mystery

ZANE GREY
The Spirit of the Border

WYATT EARP

RIN TIN TIN
Rinty
Call to Danger
The Ghost Wagon Train

WALT DISNEY
Spin and Marty
Spin and Marty, Trouble at Triple-R
Zorro

**ASSIGNMENT IN SPACE
WITH RIP FOSTER**

GUNSMOKE

WALTON BOYS
Gold in the Snow

RED RYDER
Adventure at Chimney Rock

ANNIE OAKLEY
Ghost Town Secret
Double Trouble

TRIXIE BELDEN
The Mysterious Visitor
Mystery in Arizona

NOAH CARR, YANKEE FIREBRAND

LEE BAIRD, SON OF DANGER

DONNA PARKER
At Cherrydale
Special Agent
On Her Own

FURY
The Lone Pine Mystery

LASSIE
Mystery at Blackberry Bog
The Secret of the Summer

CIRCUS BOY
Under the Big Top
War on Wheels

BOBBSEY TWINS
Merry Days Indoors and Out
At the Seashore
In the Country

CHEYENNE
The Lost Gold of Lion Park

WELLS FARGO
Danger Station

Adventure! Mystery! Read these exciting
stories written especially for young readers